DEATH A LA BANQUE

She had come to Reno to shed a few problems —and an unwanted husband, and she wiled away her waiting time in the lush casinos and exotic night spots—making a little money, acquiring an admirer or two, and—as it turned out—a couple of very deadly enemies. For, before she realized how treacherously certain Reno people played any game, there were two very dead bodies decorating the scene and a double murder rap laid invitingly at her feet.

"Leslie Ford knows how to write mystery novels"   —NEW YORK TIMES

ABOUT THE AUTHOR

LESLIE FORD has become one of the most widely read mystery writers in America. Her first novel was published in 1928 and since then she has written over fifty others.

Reno Rendezvous

by Leslie Ford

WILDSIDE PRESS

Reno Rendezvous

Published by Wildside Press LLC
www.wildsidepress.com

Reno
Rendezvous

1

Out of the enormous white letters scattered over the smooth
dun-colored mountains of Nevada—as if some petulant giant
baby had chucked the whole alphabet out of his soup—I at
long last spotted the "R" that stands for Reno. But not before the blonde girl in black had put her tiny veil down from
her smart close-fitting black straw hat and gathered her handsome silver foxes on her arm. It was the first move
she'd made, except to order a sandwich she'd hardly touched.
Through half a dozen states she had not turned her eyes
from the tiny window at her side. The merry quips that even
sensible people can't resist making at the merest mention of
Reno, and that the other passengers, all men, had been toss-
ing off since one of them had asked me where I was going,
had left her cold. We knew she was going there too; her
parchment bag said so. And she looked it, some way—the set
of her round jaw and the droop at the corner of her hard red
mouth, and her fixed gaze out of the window.

I'd been wondering about her, across the shining green
corn carpet of Nebraska, wondering if this was another of
what people call the tragedies of Reno. Not that she looked
particularly tragic, or even unhappy for that matter. She
looked moody and disturbed, but on the whole more like a
gal who knew what she wanted and was jolly well on her way
to get it than like any frail blossom broken by the iron heel
of Life. Would Judy Bonner be like this, I wondered? . . .
and for the three hundredth time, I suppose, since I'd got it
two days before, I took out the cable that was bringing me,
Grace Latham, widow—by act of God, not Court—to Reno
instead of to Maine to spend the summer with my two boys
as originally planned. It was from London, from my brother-
in-law. From my husband's sister Mildred's husband, to be
precise.

"Judith in Reno divorcing Clem," I read. "Urgently beg
you go out and try make her listen to reason. Mildred in
state of collapse. Nothing gained by her going out which she
insists doing unless you agree go. Reports from Reno disquieting. Beg you go at once great favor me and Mildred."

And I was going—but the favor, if any, was to Judy, not
her parents. I didn't know what had happened to take Judith

7

Bonner—twenty-two, and married three years—to Reno. I
did know very well that it wouldn't help to have her mother,
who is probably the most charming and utterly silly woman
in the world, out there in one of her periodic states of collapse, trying to persuade Judy to listen to reason. That in itself sounded pretty ominous. I'd never, some way, thought
of reason and Judy in the same breath, or dreamed her parents would . . . though in the years I've known her I've
been from time to time almost reduced to tears by her sudden young sweetness, and her almost childlike loyalty and
honesty, and the stanch passionate little spirit that she wears
like a banner.

—And Clem, I wondered again? Her mother had collapsed
because she married him, and was now collapsing because
she was divorcing him. What could have happened? How
would he be taking this? He'd been married and divorced
before he married Judy. That was part of the disgrace that
had reduced Judy's mother to the point where she'd had to
take a six months' cruise around the world to put her on her
feet again. Though that divorce hadn't been Clem Bonner's
fault—or so I'd always understood. In fact I remembered,
as well as if it had been the day before, Judy standing in
front of the marble fireplace in her parents' apartment overlooking Central Park, her chin up, her red-gold curls tossed
back, her wide-set sea-gray eyes dark shining pools, saying
quietly, "I'm sorry, Mother—but I'm going to marry him. I
love him . . . and I do know what it means. It means everything's all different, and everything I've ever done seems
stupid, and empty. And he's all there is! Oh, don't you *see!*"

I still remember her mother, weeping in the corner of the
sofa: "But, Judy . . . he's *divorced!*"

And Judy, the light of heaven in her lovely sun-gold face,
passionately loyal, defending him. "But it wasn't his fault,
Mother! She only married him because his family had money,
and when they lost it she left him cold—just walked out on
him! Everybody knows that. She married again the minute
she got her divorce—the papers were full of it!"

And I could still see Judy's father, haggard and upset,
torn between the two of them. "We only want you to be
happy, Judy . . . not to make a mess of your life!"

"I'm not going to make a mess of it! The mess would be if
I didn't! I love him—and I'm going to marry him! Nobody
can stop me!"

And nobody could. They drove down to Elkton in Mary-
land and got one of those people with the lighted signs on
their lawn—"MINISTER, MARRIAGE LICENSE"—out of bed
at two in the morning.

So that's why I was going to Reno . . . not to try to reason with her, but to keep her mother, who can collapse from anything from sudden death to underdone soufflé, from trying to do it; for I couldn't believe that a marriage like that could go on the rocks without leaving bitter heartache.

It seems strange now the way it all worked out. I'm sure I didn't, when I left Washington, have the slightest inkling that anything more serious than domestic tragedy was waiting for me beyond the plains. I did telephone Colonel John Primrose, 92nd Engineers, U. S. Army, Retired, the night before I left; but I only did it because he was in San Francisco, as special agent for the Treasury Department on a counterfeiting case, and getting ready to leave for home. I hoped when I did it that he and not his man Friday—if that's not too frivolous a thing to call Phineas T. Buck, First Sergeant 92nd Engineers, U. S. A., Retired—would answer the phone. But things don't happen that way, not in my life. When I heard Sergeant Buck answer, it didn't take television for me to see his lantern-jawed granite pan congeal and his dead fish-gray eyes narrow as he recognized my voice. Nor did his sinister tones saying "I'll call the Colonel, ma'am," in any way conceal the fact that he was thinking bitterly that not even a continent between us was sufficient to keep his Colonel from my designing clutches. For Sergeant Buck has long been convinced that no widow of thirty-eight can meet a man—any man, but especially one as engaging as his Colonel, even if he has successfully avoided the shoals of matrimony for fifty-one years—and not have definitely dishonorable intentions.

And, of course, for her to telephone from the East Coast that she'd be in Reno in three days, and do stop and see her, was just to confirm Sergeant Buck's worst fears and most horrible imaginings. I knew that from Colonel Primrose's chuckle coming over three thousand miles of wire, and wished instantly that I hadn't been so stupid, and had let them pass me somewhere in Nebraska, and given Sergeant Buck the pleasure of finding me gone when they got home. I was even sorrier I hadn't, a day or so later.

The blonde girl put on her gloves. The plane bounced gently, and taxied steadily to a stop. Outside, the hot desert air struck like a draft from a blast furnace. I stood there for an instant, a little bewildered in the general confusion. It seemed curious to me then, and I never did get used to it, about Reno, how so comparatively few people could make so much turmoil. There weren't more than seven or eight there, milling about, all lit in varying degrees, shouting and screaming, waving good-bye to a girl with a spray of bat-

tered gardenias long enough for a gangster's funeral on her
shoulder. She was rather tighter than the rest.

The co-pilot grinned at me.

"Just an old Reno custom," he said tolerantly.

I learned he was right, even to the sheaf of brown-edged
gardenias tied with silver ribbon, a sort of reverse bridal
bouquet, and the shouting and laughing and kissing farewell
as they shoved a free woman onto the plane, almost before
the blonde girl and I were properly debouched.

Not, however, before I heard her glad cry: "Dex! Darling!
How *marvellous!*"

And there she was, silver foxes, veil and all, in the arms
of a tall handsome chap, booted and spurred, in an elegant
flaming red satin shirt and blue jeans tucked into the tops of
a pair of fancy high-heeled Western boots.

"Kaye—darling!"

The man called Dex held her at arms' length and looked
up and down her slim smart figure.

"You look like a million! But you'd better get the city
clothes off, or they'll have you in the jug!"

I scrambled around for my luggage.

"Hotel Washoe, miss?"

An odd-looking colored man, also in a red satin shirt
(rayon, this time) and a cowboy hat, broke through the milling crowd and grabbed my bag. Somebody took down the
steps, and the big red and silver plane roared away, and the
little crowd around went suddenly flat. Like a New Year's
Eve party when you wonder, all of a sudden, what you're
shouting about, and wish you were home in bed where it's
quiet. At least that's the way I feel, on New Year's parties,
and after having been in Reno a week it's certainly the way
I feel about divorce parties. Except that the let-down is worse.
It didn't occur to me then, as it always did later, that the
girl flying away over the dun-colored mountains had quit
laughing too, and the faint nausea in the pit of her stomach
wasn't entirely due to the sudden rising from the earth.

But I didn't think about that then. All I thought about was
that the deflated little crowd of people in circus clothes was
moving away. Somebody said, "Oh God, if I don't get a drink
I'm going to die," and that seemed to put a little life into them
again.

"I'm taking Kaye in," the man called Dex said. "The rest
of you can get in with Whitey."

He tossed the blonde girl's bag into a dark green coupé
standing there. Considering what that car came to mean to
me in the next few days, it's surprising I didn't notice then

that it was custom-made, with yellow leather seats and a tortoise-shell wheel, and carried New York license plates.

"Hey—where's the old lady?" the man they called Whitey shouted from the big open car that all the rest of them had piled into. He was a bandy-legged little man in tan jodhpurs and a salt-sack polo shirt, and his hair, eyes and eyelashes were so blond that he was practically albino.

Dex shrugged. "Dunno. Must have missed the plane."

Then one girl in Whitey's car got out. I saw her say something to the rest of them, and both cars vanished in a cloud of dust. She came swiftly across the sand to me—a slight, willowy girl with dark chestnut curls cropped close to her head, nice dark eyes, and no makeup except the scarlet lips and the warm brown of the desert sun. She had on blue jeans and a white shirt open at the neck. She smiled a friendly rather shy smile. "Are you by any chance Judy Bonner's aunt Mrs. Latham?"

"Yes, I am," I said.

She laughed a little.

"The rest of them said you were too young—you were just another customer out for a divorce," she said. "I'm Polly Wagner. I'm a friend of Judy's. She asked us to meet you."

We shook hands. All the things I'd been hearing about Reno sort of evaporated. Here was another girl like Judy —not like the blonde girl on the plane.

I smiled with some relief. "Where is Judy?" I asked.

Her dark eyes clouded just a little.

"I'll go in with you, part way," she said. She held the door of the Hotel Washoe's lumbering old limousine open and we got in, while my colored cowboy labored to get it started, the perspiration making large spots on his rayon satin shirt.

She gave me a quick little smile.

"Judy's perfectly all right," she said. "I don't mean she's not. But . . . you know, Reno's an awfully funny place. It does odd things to people, if—well, if they're unhappy. And Judy is, even if she'd rather die than admit it."

I didn't say anything. Polly Wagner, who didn't look a day older than sixteen, flushed.

"Please don't think I'm barging in on Judy's private life. But I . . . well, she's such a perfectly swell person I hate to see her sort of . . . oh, you know how when you're hurt and bewildered, and all that, you try to pretend you're having a grand time, and you dance all night just because you can't bear to go to bed and be by yourself to think, and you're too proud to just go in a corner and die."

"Is that what Judy's doing?" I asked quietly.

"Well, not exactly. But—she's staying in town. Most girls like her go out to one of the good ranches. I'm at Sun Mountain Ranch. But she was out one night and went back. It was so quiet she couldn't stand it."

"You seem to be standing it," I said. I looked at her eager young face that certainly had nothing tragic or unhappy in it.

She smiled again. "That's different. You see, I'm like about ninety per cent of the people who come out here. They know they're going to marry somebody they're awfully in love with before they come. They've made a mess of one marriage and everything's ahead of them. The ranch is marvellous then, because you've got time to think, and you've got something awfully swell to think about. The other ten per cent just have a mess behind and nothing ahead. The desert's empty and . . . desolate, then. Me, for instance—I'm going to marry a man I adore, and I've had a perfectly rotten five years. So I . . . I love the desert, and the mountains, and the . . . the peace. I don't get any kick out of gambling and night clubs."

"And Judy does?"

"That's the point," she said quickly. "She doesn't. She hates it all. But she's got to do something to keep her mind off . . . off things. Oh, you know how it is, don't you? It's why Paris was so gay during the war."

"Yes, I know," I said. I wondered vaguely where she'd heard that. She must have been a babe in arms when Paris was so gay.

She turned her open friendly young face earnestly to mine.

"What I mean is, don't . . . don't be surprised at people like Dex Cromwell, and the rest of them—and don't let her do anything she'll be sorry for when she gets away from here . . ."

"Who is Dex Cromwell?" I asked.

She looked a little embarrassed.

"He was the man back there with the red shirt and the green car, who took the other woman off the plane."

"Oh," I said. "And does everybody always dress as if he belonged to a circus?"

She laughed.

"That's just for the rodeo. But if it isn't the rodeo it's something else. It helps people forget their troubles."

She looked at the watch on her brown wrist.

"I'll get out here and wait for the station wagon to Sun Mountain."

My cowboy chauffeur drew up beside the gray walls of the

Nevada Stock Farm on the main road. Polly Wagner started to get out. Then she turned back to me.

"What's Clem Bonner like?"

I looked a little surprised, I suppose. "Hasn't Judy told you?"

She shook her head.

"She never mentions him, and when everybody else starts telling what perfectly swell people their husbands are—so you wonder why on earth they're getting a divorce until you find out that's part of the Reno pattern—Judy always leaves. I think she's still frightfully in love with him. I just wondered what sort of a person he is."

"I should have thought he was perfectly grand," I said. "I like him a lot. This divorce is all bewildering to me."

"There's your car, miss."

The chauffeur pointed to a station wagon coming along the road. Polly dashed out and stood in the road, waving one hand to them and the other to me. A nice-looking girl driving drew up to take her in. There were five others in the back, all in the clothes people wear at dude ranches, all charming and all laughing . . . and all of them, I thought, remembering what Polly had just told me, belonging to the ninety per cent, with life ahead of them.

I nodded to the driver. I had better get on, it occurred to me, to Judy Bonner of the ten per cent—whose life had stopped, and whose future was only a bewildering memory of the past.

2

Until I'd got that cablegram I now had in my bag, I had in some quite normal way entirely escaped the phenomenon of Reno. A lot of my friends were divorced, of course, but usually the time element hadn't been urgently important, and when it had been they'd gone to Paris where they could get some clothes at the same time, not Nevada. I'd heard about Reno, about its divorce dens and the open flaunting of its sin and shame, and all the rest of it, but the only very clear picture I had in mind was of apparently respectable lawyers standing with their famous movie star clients in front of a classical-porticoed court house looking rather smugly pompous. Then on the plane coming out a plumbing salesman had

called it The Boulevard of Broken Dreams, and another salesman had showed me a piece in a sensational magazine calling
it The Sodom of the West.

It looked like any other small Southwestern town as we
rolled along past the Nevada Stock Farms, a series of pigmy
post offices in gray stone with a beautiful sleek Palomino
looking over the fence, and down the highway past fruit
stands and neat white-fenced houses set in groves of silver-
backed cottonwoods—except, of course, for the enormous
billboards advertising penny roulette and various hot spots
where one dined and danced and gambled. Then it changed
as we came closer to the town; it was more prosperous, and
busier, as we came into Virginia Street with its elaborate
garages and service stations, and the Washoe County court
house with its green velvet lawn accented with spears of scarlet cannas, and the Riverside Hotel on one side, and on the
other the shady public park in front of the Auditorium, and
the handsome new post office, and then, between the post
office and the Truckee River, Reno's other fashionable hotel,
the Washoe.

The limousine turned in, a doorman in a purple rayon shirt
and blue denims and a kelly-green handkerchief took my
bag.

"Hello," he said. "You just come?"

I said, "Yes."

"Well," he said, "you'll like it here when you get used to
it."

I said, "I'm sure I will."

A frightful din of cowbells and honking of horns came up
the blazing hot street, fighting with the roar of the steam
shovel that I could see tearing at the rocky bed of the
Truckee River. A second doorman, dressed in blue denims
and a purple rayon shirt with a kelly-green kerchief at his
neck, took my bag.

"Just come?" he shouted.

I nodded.

"You'll like it when you get used to it!" he bellowed.

"I'm sure I will!" I shouted back . . . momentarily surer
that I certainly wouldn't.

He put my bag down in front of the desk. The clerk wore
a bright red rayon shirt with a brighter yellow kerchief. "You
register from Reno," he said politely.

I must have looked as bewildered as I felt.

"You register from Reno. There—where it says 'Address'."

I know I looked definitely feeble-minded. He smiled as at
an especially low-grade child, and said patiently, "You regis-

ter from Reno—to establish yourself as a permanent resident of Nevada."

I said, "Oh," blankly.

He frowned, a definite glint of suspicion coming into his eye.

"You are here for a divorce, aren't you?"

I had the dreadful feeling that I was being subversive—like going to a party during Prohibition days and refusing a drink. He looked at me very much the way one's host would have looked then, as if you were plainly implying the liquor was so much poison, and said "Oh."

"I'm here to stay with Mrs. Bonner," I explained hastily, and rather apologetically, I'm afraid.

The change was instant.

"Oh, of course—you're Mrs. Latham, Mrs. Bonner's aunt. We thought you'd be somewhat older, Mrs. Latham.—But you're expected!"

He didn't actually waggle his finger at me, but almost, and he positively trilled the last part of the sentence.

"Jack!"

He summoned a bell hop with black sleeked-down hair, also done up in cowboy boots and blue jeans. "Take Mrs. Latham's bags up to 308, adjoining Mrs. Bonner's apartment, and open the connecting door.—Thank you, Mrs. Latham!"

I followed Jack to the elevator. The girl running it had on frontier pants and boots and a pink shirt, and she was chewing gum.

"Mrs. Bonner's gone riding," she said. "Who'd she go with, Jack?"

Jack shook his head. "Dunno," he said. "Some new guy I never saw before."

The girl smiled reassuringly at me.

"She'll be back pretty soon," Jack said. "Did you look in the bar? That's the place to look in if you want to find anybody in Reno.—Did you see who just blew in?"

For a startled instant I thought he was still talking to me, but he wasn't. The elevator girl said, "Do you mean the blonde with the silver foxes?"

He nodded. "That's Kaye Gorman. Baby, did she burn this joint up when she was here three years ago!"

"That was before I came," the girl said. "But she's sure going to town with Mr. Cromwell."

She laughed an odd little laugh. In the narrow oblong mirror in front of her I saw the warning wink the bell hop gave her, and the sudden scared look in her eyes as she brought the car to with a jolt at the third floor. I didn't need to be psychic to realize that Kaye Gorman was the blonde girl who had stared moodily out the window of the plane all morning . . . or to see, as clearly as if it had been written on the elevator wall, that this was something that involved Judy Bonner.

That sentence in her father's cablegram—"Reports from Reno disquieting"—flashed into my mind, more disturbing than anything I'd heard from Polly Wagner. And it wasn't five minutes later—when my bell hop had flung up the windows in my room, opened the door to Judy's apartment, pocketed his tip and got rather hurriedly out—that I saw, on the chromium and glass table in the center of her charming rose-and-gray sitting room, the gossip sheet of one of the more sensational New York papers, with flamboyant red crayon marks all over it. I picked it up. It had a photograph of Judy Bonner in a white low-cut evening frock, seated at a roulette table with what seemed to me a very large stack of chips in front of her, laughing and having a grand time, while over her bare shoulder, in black tie and dinner jacket, leaned the man I'd seen meeting Kaye Gorman at the airport.

The photograph was captioned "Playboy Meets Girl?" Below it, heading the daily gossip column, was the following:

"Will the lovely Judith Bonner, now doing time in the divorce capital, take another chance at the wheel of matrimony with Playboy Dex Cromwell when she's free?

"Rumor, which tells the truth—like a lot of well-known liars—when you least expect it, has it that Clem Bonner, who's been given the air by the beautiful Judy, will patch it up with the first Mrs. Bonner again . . . now that she's free . . . with one-third (dower right) of the four million dollar fortune of the tobacco king who dropped dead at the Kentucky Derby last year. Maybe that's what they were talking about so earnestly at Armand's opening the other night (Picture on Page 4.)"

I turned to Page 4. Smiling up at me, under the caption "Widow of Tobacco King Does the Hot Spots," was the girl whose unsmiling sullen profile I'd been looking at ever since we'd left Omaha that morning. It said below: "Kaye Gorman, former show girl, widow of Lem Gorman, well-known sportsman who dropped dead at the Kentucky Derby, on her first appearance since the tobacco magnate's death. Her first husband was Clem Bonner, whose second wife, Judith Bonner, is in Reno getting a divorce."

I am not normally a drinking woman, but I poured myself a stiff shot of scotch from a half-empty bottle on the lacquer-and-chromium bar built neatly in between the long windows and drank it practically straight. Then I stepped out on the narrow balcony into the sun, and stood leaning weakly against the terra cotta balustrade, looking down into the Truckee River, thinking—for the first time in the twenty years I'd known Judy's mother—that she had a good and sufficient reason to be in a real state of collapse . . . whether she knew it or not.

Then quite suddenly it dawned on me, standing there, why Judy hadn't met me at the plane, why she'd had her friends meet me, why she'd been out riding when I got to the hotel. She'd left the paper, open and red-marked, where I'd have to see it, see it before I saw her . . . not knowing whether I knew all the gossip and rumor that was flying about or not. I felt a sharp sting of pity. What would she do—brazen it out? Or wasn't there anything, really, to brazen out? Was it just that Clem Bonner was going back to the blonde girl he'd married his last year in Harvard, and she was letting him go? Or was it all something quite else? Was Polly Wagner right in thinking she was still desperately in love with Clem? And if so, did that explain Dex Cromwell . . . ?

But chiefly—and I think, looking back on it, it's what actually was worrying me more than anything else—what was Kaye Gorman, Clem's first wife, doing in Reno? She'd divorced Clem there, but that had been almost four years before. And it couldn't have been the climate that brought her back. It was hardly fit for anything but a salamander.

I balanced my empty glass on the balcony rail and stared down on the flag-decked streets, sharp and objective there in the brilliant scorching sun. The air was as crystal-clear as the shallow swift-running water of the narrow river, and as heady as fine champagne. Ander the red and yellow and white and blue pennants strung over the streets, the people, dressed in Western clothes as unrestrained as the decorations, moved gaily, dodging in and out among cars parked at angles against the curbs. An old man on a pinto pony leading a procession of small children on ponies of varying sizes paraded solemnly down the middle of the street toward the Park. And somewhere in all this carnival town—The Biggest Little City in the World, the street sign said—was Judy Bonner.

"Did you look in the bar?" the bell hop had asked. I glanced back at the array of half-empty bottles on the cocktail bar between the windows, and thought of that picture of Judy with the stack of chips at the roulette wheel, the man bending down over her, almost touching her bare shoulder.

In the street below me a sudden appalling din rose over the crashing roar of the steam shovel in the River. A crowd collected around a big gray truck with bars like a jail, with horns honking and cowbells clattering uproariously. I saw a woman in white being hustled up the steps and inside the truck with several other women.

"That's the Kangaroo Court," a voice near me said. "They put you in it and fine you a box at the rodeo, if you haven't got something Western on."

I looked around. A man in well-cut riding breeches and a white shirt open at the neck was standing in the next little balcony, about ten feet from me.

"Oh," I said.

"You've just come, haven't you?"

I nodded.

"For the cure?"

I looked blank.

"That's what they call getting a divorce," he said, and I said "Oh" again.

He laughed. He had several gold teeth that showed when he opened his mouth, and there was something about him—about his sun-tanned baldish head and about his eyes, the whites slightly bloodshot and the lower lids a little puffy, and about the way he looked at me, that wasn't awfully attractive.

"Did you come on the plane?" he asked.

I nodded.

"Well, let me give you a tip. Don't trust anybody in this hole. They're all out to get your money. That's all they care about. Be careful of your lawyer's wife, just for instance, if she invites you out to dinner and a little game. Don't go—not if you don't want to be taken for a couple of hundred before the evening's over."

He flicked his cigarette into the air and watched it hit the water.

"My name's Ewing, Steve Ewing," he said. "I'll be glad to take you around till you know the ropes. I'm getting my divorce in a couple of weeks. I wouldn't have come out here for it, but my wife and I haven't lived together for eight years, so I just decided to get it over with quick. Let her marry him."

He shrugged.

"I suppose you're like all the rest—getting married again the minute you get your decree?"

I swallowed. "I'm not getting—"

"You're wise, Mrs. Latham—very wise," he said earnestly. I hadn't had a chance to say I wasn't getting a divorce, and I was so startled at his knowing my name that I didn't try to correct him.

He laughed again.

"You see I know your name—I asked the elevator girl who you were."

He leaned over his balcony and fixed his eyes earnestly on mine.

"You won't believe it, little lady, but you're the first woman I've seen out here that I wanted to look at twice."

He shrugged again.

"I go around, of course. A man can't just sit in his room all day. But I'm fed up with the girls you see here. Bar flies —nothing but bar flies. I'd given up, absolutely, till I saw you get out of the elevator just now. Do you know, that one minute changed my whole life?"

I'm afraid I stared at him quite open-mouthed. He leaned closer over the pink terra cotta balustrade.

"You won't mind, will you, if I can't help feeling sorry for your husband, poor devil—and glad there's no lucky man I've got to start hating before I've ever seen him?"

"Do be careful," I said weakly. He was leaning at an alarming angle over the rail.

"My dear, I've already fallen so hard a few hundred feet wouldn't make the least difference."

If I'd ever thought that being a widow had taught me poise in such a situation, I was quite wrong. I simply stared at him. I had no way of realizing, of course, that this was a most harmless and naïve example of how fast people work in Reno. They usually say it's the altitude, and perhaps it is. I wouldn't know.

"Would you like another drink?" Mr. Ewing said. He was looking at the glass in my hand.

"No, thanks," I said hurriedly. "I've got to go unpack."

"Then I'll see you in the lobby in . . . shall we say, half an hour?"

He gave me what I imagine was intended for a seductive glance, and said, "Do you know, I've been looking for you all my life . . . and isn't it strange I should find you in Reno, of all places?"

"It certainly is," I said. I staggered back into Judy's sitting room and sank down on the gray-and-rose sofa, and put my glass on the floor.

3

"You'll like it when you get used to it," the doorman in the fancy dress had said. All I could think of was that if this certainly very startling thing had happened to me at the advanced age of thirty-eight, what must Judy Bonner have walked into—being twenty-two, and beautiful, and rich, and heralded by half-a-dozen nationally read columnists? Was this Dex Cromwell, I wondered, in his satin shirt and white Stetson, just a superior Steve Ewing she'd met in some bar?

I glanced at the paper again, at the picture of Kaye Gorman—the smiling relict of a tobacco king, with all the rights, privileges and funds thereto pertaining. Where, I wondered, would she have known Dex Cromwell so well? His "Kaye, darling! You look like a million!" should really have been "a million and a third," I thought suddenly . . . not knowing that in that thought the deadly virus of Reno had already infected me and that I was just running true to form on the inside of the track.

I picked up the paper and stuffed it into the waste basket, and put my glass on the bar. Then, without waiting to unpack, I went down to the lobby. My friend Steve Ewing was there already, with his arm around a girl in light blue shorts and dark glasses, helping her write a telegram. I slipped around something that looked like an old-fashioned tub of palms except that it had chromium bands and was painted Chinese red, and followed a neon arrow that said "Cocktail Lounge."

The noise would have been enough without the arrow, although as a matter of fact there weren't a lot of people there. Most of it came from a three-piece orchestra of young men in blue jeans—Levi's, I learned they're called—with bright kerchiefs (which my young, brought up in the effete East, refer to as oatmeal-catchers) round their necks and wearing three more of the gaudy rayon shirts. They were on a triangular dais set in one corner of the big room. The bar, an elaborate affair of crystal and chromium and Chinese red, flanked them on the left, a battery of gaming tables on the right. The roulette wheel and the crap table were empty. An oldish man in ordinary clothes and a perfectly stunning girl, with curly blue-black hair and white skin, dressed in white riding breeches and black boots and a white satin shirt, were playing at the twenty-one table.

Opposite the orchestra, along the wall on either side of the door where I was standing, were more slot machines than I'd ever seen before, anywhere, though not nearly as many as I was to see practically daily for the next few weeks. A middle-aged woman in an extraordinary outfit that was a combination of Pocahontas and the Girl of the Golden West was methodically stuffing dimes into one of them and pulling the lever without any apparent benefit to herself. She glanced at me as I came in.

"Nobody but a damned fool," she remarked calmly, "would waste his time on these machines."

She gave me a quick smile from a pair of shrewd merry blue eyes above a fine aquiline nose and brightly rouged lips. Her hair, cropped and waved, may have been auburn once and was certainly henna now, and her face, which must have been astonishingly lovely, was still very handsome, if a little stamped with a lifetime of determination. She was all in all —except possibly for the Western getup—rather the sort of person you'd expect to see entertaining a diplomat at the Sulgrave Club than pulling the handle of a slot machine in a hotel bar in Reno.

She fished a five-dollar bill out of her bag and summoned the waiter. "Here, Eddie—get me some more dimes. I bet I've put a hundred dollars in these crooked machines of yours."

Eddie, bald and wrinkled yet oddly juvenile, like some very ancient little boy, grinned and trotted toward the bar, and I went on in . . . because, in a brief lull, I'd heard a voice that I'd come three thousand miles to hear. Just as I stepped in, I saw, in one of the mirrored columns that give the cocktail lounge at the Hotel Washoe an extent and crowded gaiety that it doesn't have, a slim girl in riding clothes, with red-gold hair in a long loosely-waved bob around her sun-browned throat, rise suddenly from a crowd of people around a low table, in front of a curving red leather seat under the windows at the far end of the bar.

A man's voice said, "Aw' sit down, Judy—what the hell!"

I think I should have recognized it as the voice of the man they'd called Whitey at the airport even if I hadn't seen him half rise and take the glass out of my niece's hand.

Another voice said, "Don't go Eastern on us, Judy."

I saw Dex Cromwell pull himself elegantly to his feet and stand, looking down into her suddenly upturned face in a way that I suppose was intended to be humorous and masterful, at the same time. And it apparently was, for I saw Judy's stiff little back suddenly crumple.

"Oh, I'm sorry!" she said, with a short odd laugh that

seemed so unlike the girl I knew that I was really disturbed.

She picked up her cocktail glass and emptied it and set it down. Nobody had said anything for an instant. They were all watching her. As I came up I saw that Kaye Gorman was sitting there, watching her too, her eyes a curious cat-green in a face that otherwise was as near expressionless as a wax doll's.

Nobody had noticed me coming toward them. Not until I said, "Hello, Judy."

For an instant Judy Bonner's lithe figure, taller and slimmer in trim brown jodhpurs than I'd remembered it, stiffened, perfectly taut. Then she whirled around, her face the oddest mixture of the most conflicting emotions . . . surprise, and hurt, and something else that I shouldn't have noticed, I'm afraid, except for the way she blinked suddenly, fighting to keep back the tears.

She didn't say a word. She took one step to where I was standing and grabbed hold of my arm and held it in hers.

Then she turned around to the man behind her.

"Dex!" she cried. "You told me she didn't get off the plane!"

Mr. Dexter Cromwell gave me one surprised look. Then his handsome face wrinkled in the most engaging mock despair.

"But Judy—you said your *aunt!* We saw this lady—but we thought she was just another customer, out for the cure. She doesn't look like anybody's aunt . . . not even yours, darling!"

He stepped forward and put out his hand with a frank charming smile. "How do you do, Mrs. Latham! You really don't, you know—look like anybody's aunt!"

"Well, I might feel flattered," I said, "—if I hadn't seen you so instantly engrossed with my fellow passenger."

It was a perfectly horrid thing to say, I suppose, especially as I had heard Whitey say "Hey—where's the old lady?" And in a sense it was rather flattering that it hadn't occurred to any of them that I was she.

Dex Cromwell smiled again.

"Oh come, come, lady—let's be friends!"

He looked at Kaye Gorman.

"Rescue me, Kaye! Tell them I didn't even know you were coming out!"

The blonde girl gave him the most provokingly open smile.

"Darling—don't tell me! I thought that was what you were there for, to meet me! That's all I've been living on!"

She sipped her daiquiri, her baby blue eyes wide open above its frosted rim.

The color burned in hot dull patches under Judy's brown cheeks.

I jumped as a voice spoke in my ear. The man called Whitey had got up and was standing by me. "Look what you started," he said out of one side of his mouth. He turned to some nondescript young woman behind him. "If that ain't the payoff!" he added. "Remember I said half-way back I wondered if the dame with the Park Avenue accent was the kid's aunt?"

Somebody said, practically, "You'll wind up behind the eight ball yourself, if you don't keep out of this."

It sounded sensible to me. I was beginning to wish I'd kept out. Judy's strong brown fingers were gripping my arm like a vise. The thin edges of her perfect little nostrils were quivering.

"Let's go upstairs, Grace," she said quietly. She'd never, even when she was in pigtails, dignified me with an Aunt to my name. "So long—we'll be seeing you."

Whitey spoke suddenly as we turned to go. "Hey, take your antique, Judy. I guess that's what you call it."

Judy turned back. I looked around.

He handed her an odd-looking implement. It was a black rusty piece of wrought iron, about a foot long, that looked like a meat skewer except that at one end a hook was set in it alongside a small hollow cylinder that contained an old piece of candle dropping over the side. At the base of the short candle holder was a metal thumb piece.

"What's that?" Kaye Gorman asked curiously.

Dex Cromwell took it. "It's an old candle pick they used in the mines," he said.

Whitey fingered the sharp pointed end. "They stuck it in the timbers," he said. "Or they hung it up."

He pointed to the hook behind the candle cylinder. "You get it up in Virginia City?"

Judy nodded.

"You could kill a guy with that, Judy."

Judy nodded again.

"That's what the man at Virginia City said—and he said it wouldn't be the first time it had been used for that."

She poked the end of it into her own flat little stomach and smiled, more like the Judy I knew, all of a sudden, than she had been before. "In fact, I'd rather thought of using it myself."

Whitey grinned, looking at me. "I'll bet," he said.

Judy took my arm again. "Come along, darling," she said. We went out. I was aware of a curious silence that we left behind us, and then, out of it, I heard Kaye Gorman . . .

and with no possible hope that Judy wasn't hearing her too.
"Lord, no wonder Clem made her come out. I thought it was
only his sanity he was afraid of, but God, it's his life too!"

I felt Judy's body stiffen, her hand tighten in a little spasm
on my arm. Then she relaxed suddenly, with what seemed to
me a rather woeful attempt at sang-froid.

"I'd especially like to use it on that woman," she said.

She gripped my arm again. "Oh, I hate her, Grace—I hate
her!"

"I know, angel," I said. "But—"

She laughed. "I'm sorry! Don't pay any attention to me,
darling."

We got out of the elevator. Judy unlocked the door of her
apartment. She stood for a moment looking at the table, with
a little oddly-bewildered look, as if something she had been
dreading had escaped her. Then her eyes roved around the
room.

"If you're looking for that paper," I said, throwing my hat
on the sofa, "I put it in the waste basket."

I looked at her. Her face was crumpled, suddenly, and I
don't know what happened to the space between us, for the
next instant Judy Bonner was in my arms, crying as if her
heart would break. She was also sitting on my hat, which I'd
paid thirty-five dollars for in a mad moment in New York.

"I thought you'd seen it in Chicago, and hadn't got off the
plane, when they didn't find you," she sobbed miserably.
"And here I'd been waiting for you to come, and *she* came
instead! I . . . I just thought I couldn't bear it!"

"Oh, lamb, don't be stupid," I said. I was practically weeping myself.

She sat up and dabbed at her eyes with a wadded handkerchief she fished out of her jodhpurs pocket, and sniffled.

Then she gave me a sort of miserable smile.

"If you do that in an alley in Reno, somebody tries to sell
you dope," she said. Then she smiled again. "I always say you
can pick up useful information in the most unlikely places if
you have an open mind."

"So it seems," I said. I was glad to be able to laugh at something. "I see by the papers you've gone in for gambling—I
hope you don't do dope too."

"No," she said. Her gray eyes lighted for an instant, and
became grave again. "I keep strictly to minor vices. They say
a lot of divorcées do go in for dope, but I doubt it, unless
they did before they came. They clean the place up once in
a while—but they do everywhere, don't they?"

"They seem to," I said.

"They say Whitey takes dope."

She put her miner's candle pick, which had been sticking uncomfortably into my ribs, on the table.

"But that's one of the charming things about Reno—you can hear anything you like about anybody."

She shrugged. "Maybe Whitey does take dope, but he's been awfully decent to me. Of course you've got to watch him. He'll take you for a ride every chance he gets, so don't ever let him suggest a straight game of blackjack. He's just *naturally* crooked, and as long as you remember that, he's really a grand guy. He'd just cheat his grandmother out of her last cent, but then he'd turn around and give somebody else *his* last cent."

"I see," I said—not seeing, really. "And . . . your friend Mr. Cromwell?"

Judy's clear brow clouded. "He's all right," she said quietly.

She went abruptly to the cocktail bar and poured out a stiff jolt of scotch. In the mirror I could see her face, unhappy and bitter again. She shot the glass half-full of soda, raised it to her lips, and put it down again without touching it.

"I don't know why I do that," she said abruptly. "I don't like it."

I tried to poke my hat back into shape.

"It's universally regarded as one of the least successful ways of solving emotional problems, Mrs. Bonner," I said. I got up. "I'm sorry, Judy. I didn't realize he was such a . . . a sore point. But I'd just thought, in my old-fashioned way, that if he's to be a member of the family shortly, I'd rather like to know—if not who his great-grandfather's father was —at least where you met him. But think nothing of it, darling."

I took my bag off the table.

"Are you dining with me, or have you got a date? I can manage beautifully. I've got a thousand letters to write."

"You're coming to the River House with us," she said.

And just as I got to my door she came quickly after me.

"I'm sorry, Grace!" she whispered contritely, rubbing her nose against my shoulder. If you bring children up in stables, I suppose, you've got to expect them to act rather like horses. "I'm such a pig . . . and I don't mean to be . . . not really!"

"Pigs are quite sensible people," I said. "You aren't acting like a pig, darling. You're just being silly. But let's skip it. I don't want to know anything you don't want to tell me."

She went back to the table and stood, opening and closing the silver cigarette box.

"I've known Dex quite a while," she said, in a dull little voice. "Before I came to Reno."

She went on, not very steadily, and without raising her head.

"I . . . I said I'd marry him. Before I . . . left home."

"That's swell, then," I said.

I was far from meaning it, but I was definitely glad, nevertheless, that she hadn't just picked him up along the Boulevard of Broken Dreams . . . forgetting, for a little moment, that it's a road that stretches on to infinity, only touching Reno as it passes.

I opened my door. "Does one dress?"

She looked up and laughed, her face suddenly alive and bright again.

"Only if you think you can get your man better if you haven't got much on. Kaye Gorman'll be dressed. I'm keeping these on."

4

I'd never realized until that night what a restricted and completely mousey life I'd led. And I never realized until I got home again how utterly blissful a quiet private meal can be. On the other hand, I never ate better food, or drank better wine, or heard more amusing—and shocking—songs, or saw more diverting and totally cockeyed people, than I did at Reno's River House. It's one of the so-called divorce dens, I imagine. It's certainly a den, with its painted Moorish pillars, and lights so dim and pink that the most ageing customer looks rosy-cheeked and dewy-eyed.

Through all the extraordinary and tragic things that were lying in wait for me, and that broke with the suddenness of a Washoe Zephyr—sardonically so called by the early miners because it sprang up at the drop of a hat and was likely to level every building, church or saloon, that they managed to erect in that barren and bitter wilderness—the River House of Reno remained a haven. The five days following my arrival seem now the most harrowing I've ever spent. I would have left Reno, my hair turned white in a single night, if it hadn't been that, ghastly and unbelievable as everything was, it was still, in spots, grotesquely and unbelievably funny. As —for instance—when my old friend Sergeant Buck got himself locked in the ancient plumed and flambeaued hearse out at the race track, or the early morning when my new friend Whitey ran amok in the Washoe Bar, threatening to kick the devil out of the big butter-and-sheep man who accused him of stacking the blackjack deck, which, as a matter of fact, he had done. Or—above all—the night at the Town House in First Street when the woman at the next table pointed to her drunk and enormously owlish companion completely absorbed in a Lobster Thermidor, and said proudly to her friends, "Do you know what he's done?—*He's* re-read Anthony Adverse!"

That first night, however, was not so amusing as it was just simply difficult. It began when Judy refused to wear a jacket, and then had to send Dex Cromwell back up to her room to get it, while she introduced me as her sister out for a divorce to an old dragon in a cowboy hat who wrote gossip for some Eastern paper.

"You can sue them for libel, dear, and buy yourself a new mink coat," she explained airily.

That mood didn't last. The three of us—Dex Cromwell having returned—were sitting at a round table in a corner, eating luscious strips of Persian melon sprinkled with lime juice and white Bacardi, when I saw the muscles of Judy's throat contract sharply.

She put down her spoon and turned to Dex. "If your friend Kaye is dining with us," she said, very quietly, "I'm going home."

Dex looked over his shoulder, a curious little flicker livening in his dark eyes. I followed his glance. Kaye Gorman, in a black chiffon evening gown that was positively French eighteenth century from the waist up, clinging around her elegant figure and swirling like a ballet skirt from the knees to the floor, a fox cape over her arm, stood at the arched door of the dining room, in sharp relief against the brilliantly lighted gaming tables and curving mahogany bar outside. Her bleached blonde hair and scarlet lips, the diamond bracelets on her white arm, the diamond clip at her dress against her milky white bosom, the scene behind her, made her seem quite suddenly symbolic of the whole picture . . . in the past when it was part of the richest mining spot in the world, in the present when the values were the same but the pattern so different.

The man at her side, in cowboy clothes, might have been a miner in the old days . . . only then their positions would have been reversed; he would have had the money, she would have been the one on the make. I glanced at Judy. In her riding shirt open at the neck, with her sun-tanned skin and scarlet lips and high proud little head, she was the present only. The past had no part in her.

"I tell you, if she comes here, I'm going," she repeated

calmly. Only a person who knew the depths behind those moss-gray eyes could have heard the passion under her voice.

Dex Cromwell lifted her hand and gave it a quick playful kiss. She winced almost as if he had struck her.

"Oh, don't be stupid, darling!" he said lightly. "Don't let everybody see you're jealous! What do you care if she's marrying your husband! You're getting a divorce—be a sport!— Hi, Kaye. Hello, cowboy!"

"Hello!" Kaye Gorman said. "Hello, Judy. Is there room for a rival and friend?"

She laughed shortly.

"You know Joe, don't you, Dex—and Judy? And this is Mrs. Latham. This is Joe Lucas. He's a *real* cowboy. Never's been east of Denver."

"Or is it west of Chicago?" Dex said.

Joe Lucas, who looked well-polished and shy and rather nice, grinned boyishly.

"Ah never bin no'th of Salt Lake, anyhow," he said, in as Georgia a drawl as I ever hope to hear. "How're you, Mis' Judy? Howdy, Miz' Latham."

Judy sat there, her slim body rigid, her face perfectly expressionless, except for her eyes, black as coal.

Just then, behind us, in a blue lace evening dress, appeared the dark-haired lush-looking girl I'd seen in white riding breeches and black boots at the twenty-one table in the Washoe Bar that afternoon.

"Take your hat, cowboy?" she said. A smile dimpled in the corners of her red mouth.

Joe Lucas reddened painfully as he gave up his hat. The girl reached for Kaye Gorman's fox cape.

"I'll just keep that, Vicki," Kaye said. "It looks cold around here."

The hat check girl winked at Dex Cromwell.

"Not having trouble being too popular, are you, Mr. Cromwell?"

I didn't quite see how she managed to lean so close to him as she did. I hoped Judy didn't see the neat little pinch he gave her leg, or the slow sidelong smile she returned for it. Or maybe I hoped she did.

Kaye Gorman did.

"Up to your old tricks, darling?" she inquired coolly. "Keep your head, Vicki. It takes money to keep Dex. You couldn't do it on what you make."

Dex Cromwell grinned engagingly at her. His strong white teeth in his sun-bronzed face made him look like a toothpaste ad. As far as that went, I thought suddenly, his light wavy hair made him look like a shampoo ad, and his cigarette and white wool jacket and colored scarf (Bond Street, not Rodeo) made him look like a tobacco ad. In fact he looked like the complete answer to nearly any manufacturer's prayer . . . as well as any lady's.

"She's trying to get Judy into a scene," I thought . . . with some apprehension. But Judy smiled serenely. "What'll you have, Joe?"

"Rye an' coke for me, Mis' Judy," Joe said soberly. "Doin' any ridin' lately?" he added, with lovely tact. He turned to me. "She's sure got a sweet seat on a horse, Miz' Latham. You goin' to ride while you're here?"

"Probably," I said.

Dex Cromwell had pushed back his chair.

"Shall we dance, Judy?"

"No thanks," Judy said sweetly. "I must have sprained my ankle today."

Kaye Gorman flashed out of her chair. "Oh, this is more than I deserve!"

She laughed her short laugh as she took Dex's arm. I looked at Judy. She watched them float off with a queer twisted little smile. Then she put her napkin beside her plate.

"How about a dance, Joe?" she said. "My ankle seems to be a lot better."

Joe grinned. "Ah could give him a horse that'll break his neck, easy, Mis' Judy," he said. He got up clumsily. "Excuse us, Miz' Latham?"

I nodded. His big red hand looked strange on Judy's white-shirted little back. I watched them a moment. They were amazingly good, she in her jodhpur boots and he in high-heeled Westerns. I turned back to my cocktail of small sweet Olympia oysters and ate a couple, glad of a moment's peace, until suddenly I received a slap on the back that surprised me so much I was very glad it wasn't a Lynnhaven I had in my mouth.

It was my friend Whitey. He pulled a chair up to the table and flopped into it.

"Gee, did I get a big boot out of *that!*" he exclaimed. His white eyelashes batted with enthusiasm.

"Out of what?" I asked.

He put his head in his hands and rocked crazily back and forth, in silent mirth, until I thought he'd lost his mind.

"Out of Kaye dragging Joe over here with you folks," he said at last. "She's been out of it so long she don't know Joe's the guy which would like nothing better'n to slit Dexter's gullet for him."

"Oh," I said. "Why?"

He winked at the hat check girl, Vicki, dancing with a loud, rather intoxicated and definitely apoplectic man in his early seventies, I'd say, and who'd already, so Whitey whispered to me a little later, lost four hundred dollars at the twenty-one table.

"Vicki was Joe's girl, till Dexter chiseled in."

"Who is Vicki," I asked. "I mean, does she live here?"

She looked rather more metropolitan to me, some way.

Whitey shook his head.

"She came for her divorce and went broke, so Frenchy, which is the fellow owns the joint, gave her a job. She makes enough, but she gambles, and what she don't lose that way she sops up at the bar. So as she can't get enough ahead to get out."

"I see," I said.

He took the drink the waiter had brought for Joe, and sat there, suddenly and inexplicably in a state of complete dejection, staring moodily down into it, turning the glass round and round.

"Jeez, I got to get out of this hole," he said suddenly. "It's getting me down. I'm getting to be nothing but a goddam gigolo like the rest of 'em."

I swallowed another oyster too rapidly and stared at him. He faced me abruptly.

"Look at me!" he said. "Do I look like a come-on man for a gambling joint?"

(He included another ancient occupation.)

"Look at me—what do you think my mother would say if she saw me now? Doing Mr. Cromwell's dirty work! And what for? I ask you, what for?"

"I'm sure I wouldn't know!" I said hastily.

"To keep body and soul together!" he said. "And does he give a damn, I ask you? Does he care what happens to me? No!"

He downed Joe's drink at a gulp—and if anybody thinks a drink cannot be downed in a gulp, then he has never had a Reno drink.

"I'm clearing out. I'm going to get some sleep, and tomorrow I'm going to Cromwell, and I'm going to tell him to get someone else to do his dirty work! It burns me up!"

He got unsteadily to his feet.

"Excuse me, Mrs. Latham—but it ain't often a little punk like me meets a girl like Judy. And I'm clearing out!"

"Oh dear!" I thought.

Just then the woman with the handsome aquiline face and

red hair whom I'd seen playing the dime slot maching came in the door, and the next thing I knew Whitey was dancing with her. And the next thing he was bringing her over to my table.

"Mrs. Latham," he said, beaming cheerfully, "I want you to meet Mrs. de Courcey."

"How do you do!" Mrs. de Courcey said. She sat down. "You're Judy's aunt, aren't you. She's a terribly nice girl. I can't for the life of me see what she sees in Cromwell. All the Cromwells from the Protector down have been hounds. You must have lunch with me, my dear—I must tell you about Dexter Cromwell. I met him last year in the Islands. Tried to pretend I didn't recognize him, here. It just shows nobody ever learns, especially a woman of my age. We must have lunch, my dear. So nice seeing somebody civilized in this hellhole. It's simply awful—I adore it!—Oh, hello, Frenchy! I'd *love* to dance!"

I watched her go off. In a moment Joe and Judy came back. She looked tired and deflated, some way, as if she'd been going on her nerve and that was gone too.

"I'm going home, Grace," she said. "Do you mind?"

"Go ahead, darling," I said. "I'll finish my dinner. I'm starving."

"You can get back all right?"

"I'll try," I said. "It's all of a block and a half, isn't it?"

She bent down and gave me a quick kiss on the top of my head. "Good-bye, darling."

I looked out at the dance floor. Dex Cromwell and the glamorous Kaye were nowhere in sight. And I'd finished my coffee before they showed again.

"Where's Judy?" Dex asked. He seemed rather surprised, which convinced me he was stupider than he looked.

"I wouldn't know," I said.

"She's taken Cowboy Joe," Kaye Gorman said with her short laugh. "You'll have to put up with me for the rest of the evening . . . darling."

For an instant that was electric in intensity, their eyes met and held. Dex Cromwell shrugged his shoulders and laughed.

"My luck's still holding, I guess," he said lightly.

"I'll see you later," I said. "Good-night."

As I went out the grilled door that reminded me of the speakeasy days, the hat check girl got up from a rounding deep-cushioned recess behind a little screen of palms and followed me out into the cool night. The door closed behind us before she spoke.

"You'll probably think I'm drunk, Mrs. Latham," she said,

rather diffidently, which surprised me. "But I'm not—not very. Listen—you've got to keep Mrs. Bonner from being a damn fool."

I looked at her. Even under the slightly magenta glow of the River House sign of palm trees with well—signifying an oasis in the desert, I suppose—she looked desperately unhappy. I doubt if she was a day over twenty-three, but she looked just then almost as old as time.

"He's nothing but a first-class bastard," she said, in a dull toneless voice. "She's too decent to be chasing around with him. You got to stop her. She'll do something she'll be sorry for, first thing you know—and he's not worth it!"

A sudden passionate intensity emphasized the last words.

I stood staring at her stupidly, trying to think of something to say that wouldn't be disloyal to Judy, or too old-fashioned and naïve. I was saved the trouble. A couple of men coming out of Center Street spotted her, and she them.

"Hi, Vicki! How's the girl!" one of them shouted. I heard her rippling silvery laugh against the clink of glasses and clack of chips as the grilled door opened, and the sudden silence as it closed behind them.

When I got to the Washoe virtually the same crowd was milling about. It appeared that in Reno nobody ever went to bed. Whitey, playing blackjack with the night clerk, disengaged himself for a moment. "Judy's gone out to Truckee with Joe," he said. I nodded and went on up to my room.

5

I must have gone to sleep the moment my head touched the pillow. Judy hadn't been in her room, but I hadn't expected she would be. The night was too clear and perfect to be closed in four small prosaic walls. Her car was gone from its place on the bridge over the river. I was glad she was with Cowboy Joe—with anybody, I thought as I turned off my light, but Kaye Gorman and Dex Cromwell and the gentleman known as Whitey.

The thought was still vaguely in my mind as I woke up. Without raising my head I could see the clock on the town hall across the Truckee beyond the River House, its hands dimly pointing to three. The light from the Riverside Hotel across the street went from yellow to rose to blue and back, lighting the night air half-a-dozen times before I realized that it was voices in the next room that had waked me. I didn't in fact realize it until Judy spoke, her voice low and passionate and broken with tears.

"I'll do as I please! You needn't pretend you didn't know she was coming here! You're just trying to humiliate me—and I can't bear it!"

I think I've never heard such poignant protest torn from any human throat. All the pent-up emotion of weeks was in it. The gallant little head was down . . . the storm they'd been goading her on to all afternoon had broken at last.

I heard the low tones of a man's voice, and Judy again:

"Don't you dare say you love me . . . when you know it's her!"

I got out of bed and put on my dressing gown. Then I stopped. My first impulse had been to go in there—drawn by the real agony in those heartbroken sobs. But to go in, as I realized when I stopped to think, would only have made things worse. And it wouldn't hurt her to quarrel with him, I thought—it would get it out of her system, at least—unless, of course, she woke up the whole hotel and got another notice in the gossip columns as a result.

I went to the desk and without a psychic twinge of any kind to warn me I did perhaps the most foolish thing I ever did in my life. I wrote a note saying, "Judy dear—If you two will stop this insane quarreling now, and resume at a more seasonable hour, you will please your devoted aunt who would very much like to get some sleep." I then phoned for a bell boy, who came still in fancy dress at that ungodly hour, said "Will you kindly give this to Mrs. Bonner," and went back to bed.

I couldn't go to sleep, even though I heard Judy's door slam and a long silence ensue. I lay there thinking, about Judy and Clem, and about Kaye Gorman. It didn't make sense. Nobody who ever loved Judy could love that young woman with her bleached hair and the hard curve of her jaw from behind that melted into such a round baby face in front, and the blue eyes, wide and appealing when she wanted them to be and shrewd and cold as the devil when she wasn't on guard. And Clem Bonner *had* loved Judy—I'd have staked my life on that.

I lay there for a long time; and then I reached for the phone without turning on the light, and called Clem Bonner's apartment in New York. I'd tried to get in touch with him before I came out and hadn't been able to, and it seemed to me that now it was still more imperative. He'd just be getting up. I waited. I didn't quite know what I was going to say, except to tell him that Judy needed him, desperately, and that he couldn't let her down. But I needn't have bothered; I might as well have been talking to a stone wall.

"I'm sorry—Mr. Bonner has given orders not to be disturbed. I'll tell him you called."

And when I insisted, explaining that I was Mrs. Latham, Mrs. Bonner's aunt, in Reno, and that I demanded he at least go and tell Mr. Bonner I was on the phone, the butler said "Very good, madam," and then, a minute later, with the most infuriating imperturbability, "Mr. Bonner does not care to be disturbed, madam—good-bye."

I stared into the dead phone completely dumbfounded, and then slammed it down. "The wretched young prig," I thought angrily, "—she's jolly well lucky to get rid of him!"

When I woke up again I rang for my breakfast and got up to the last peaceful day I knew for some time. Even then I should have recognized the calm as ominous . . . the sort that, as they say, precedes the storm. I finished my breakfast, bathed and got dressed. There was no sound from Judy's room. While it was reasonable to presume that even the young have to sleep some time, I nevertheless had a vague tinge of uneasiness at her sleeping so long. The clock on the square spired tower of the Town Hall said 11:30 when I opened the connecting door and looked in.

She was lying on the sofa, still in her jodhpurs and riding shirt and shoes, her red-gold hair spreading a bright nimbus about her flushed lovely face where tear stains still showed. She was breathing as quietly and evenly as a child. My note was lying on the table.

I closed the door, took the Do Not Disturb sign off my dresser, hung it on her door, went down the hall and pressed the elevator bell.

The maid came heavily up the narrow stairs to the right of the elevator.

"Mrs. Bonner is asleep," I said. "Don't do my room either, till she wakes up, please."

She gave me a look that I suppose was long-suffering rather than malevolent, and plodded off down the hall. Halfway along she turned. "You'd better put something Western on," she said. "They'll arrest you. I'm from Chicago myself."

She went on about her business, and I went on about mine.

It was hot and brilliant in Virginia Street. I turned right onto the bridge, and stood looking down into the clear shallow water of the Truckee. It was pleasant to see a stream crystal as God intended it to be, after the turgid muddy waters of the Potomac or the Susquehanna or the Mississippi. And then, just as I'd got there, I suddenly heard the clatter of cowbells and the honking of horns, and realized with a sickening feeling out of all keeping with the carnival air around me, and out of all proportion to the thing itself, that I was about to be stuck into that ridiculous travelling pen, and paraded through the streets, at a moment when I was in anything but a Mi-Carême mood.

I saw them coming, a couple of men in cowboy clothes; there was no use trying to run. And I loathe all horseplay of the sort . . . and to be caught right in the middle of it. . . . For a moment I hated Judy, and her parents, and the whole tawdry business.

Then suddenly, out of a perfectly clear sky, I saw a yellow kerchief with a bucking bronco on one corner stuck into my hand; and a familiar and most disgusted voice said:

"Here, ma'am, take this, and hang on to it. You ought to had sense enough to get one."

My fingers closed gratefully and weakly on it as I stared up at Sergeant Phineas T. Buck, guard, philosopher and friend extraordinary to my friend Colonel John Primrose, 92nd Engineers, U. S. A., Retired. He was standing there beside me, his granite visage as expressionless yet bleak as the side of a canyon in December, his viscid gray eyes fixed on me with the fine enthusiasm of a dead fish. Sergeant Buck's six-feet-three and two hundred and twenty pounds of bone and brawn, with his hard-bitten, lantern-jawed and always slightly menacing face on top of it, makes him an extraordinary figure at any time . . . but in Western clothes he was wonderful to behold. He wore cowboy pants—blue levis— and a bright orange satin shirt, and a waistcoat made of the brown-and-white-spotted skin of a calf, or something, and peculiarly fancy boots, and a wide leather belt with "RENO" studded on it in what he later referred to as stimulated rubies, and ten-gallon hat that would have held at least twenty. On it there was a gorgeous wide yellow silk band that said "Winnemucca Rodeo"—why, I never knew.

"Oh, thank you!" I gasped. Then, as I have nothing to say to Sergeant Buck that he'd care to hear, and as he would greatly prefer never to see me at all, much less speak to me, we just stood there while the Kangaroo Court, full of sheepish women in Eastern clothes, clattered by, respecting my Western insignia.

Sergeant Buck turned and spat precisely into the river.

"I expect we'll be seeing you again, ma'am," he said, out of one corner of his mouth. There was no mistaking how he felt about that inevitability.

"Well, I'm afraid so," I said. He started off. I should have liked to ask him where Colonel Primrose was, but I didn't dare. It so plainly would just have confirmed a deep-seated conviction that his chief's freedom wasn't worth a moment's purchase, and that before he got away from Reno he'd be as firmly and irrevocably bound as the lassoed steer rolling in the dust on the corner of my yellow handkerchief.

Then I noticed that Sergeant Buck had stopped a step or so away from me, and I turned, wondering if it was conceivable that he was about to mention the Colonel of his own free will and volition.

He was not even thinking about me. He was staring straight ahead of him toward the Riverside Bar, the expression on his face quite indescribable.

I followed his gaze, and wasn't surprised, much. Mrs. de Courcey, in her Pocahontas getup, her henna hair flaming in the sun, hat in hand, a brace of dachshunds on the leash, was holding up traffic crossing from the Hotel Washoe to the Riverside.

"Well, may I be a son of a . . . gun!" Sergeant Buck said slowly, out of the corner of his mouth.

He took off his mammoth hat, and mopped his brow with a red bandanna handkerchief.

Astonishing as Mrs. de Courcey was, I thought, she wasn't so astonishing as all that. I started to say so, but Sergeant Buck silenced me.

"You got to excuse me, ma'am," he said. "I been figuring it was you we come up here to see. But I guess I got him all wrong."

"What *are* you talking about?" I demanded—in my innocent way having been figuring the same thing.

He jerked his head toward Mrs. de Courcey, whose dachshunds had got tangled up with the silver spurs on her Western boots.

"Her," he said grimly. "She's an old flame of the Colonel's. He was drunk a week when she married de Courcey."

We both watched her disappear into the Riverside Bar.

"So that's the way it is," Sergeant Buck said, more grimly still. It was the first time I'd ever heard him use one of the Colonel's pet phrases. The punctuation was his own; he turned and spat again into the Truckee. "Good-bye, ma'am," he said.

I thought for a moment that it was another ruse in Sergeant Buck's efforts to keep Colonel Primrose out of my designing hands. But watching him lumber down the street in his movie costume I realized that it wasn't, and that a real and formidable danger had risen, now that Mrs. de Courcey was about to be a free woman again. I even felt a sudden glow of something like sympathy for Sergeant Buck—the situation, from his point of view, was certainly complicated.

And then, for a moment, and in spite of the fact that the idea of my marrying Colonel Primrose has never been in anybody's mind but Buck's, I felt a twinge of—I suppose—just old-fashioned jealousy. We all, no doubt, have our little vanity.

I might have brooded longer on the wound mine had got if I hadn't just then seen the hat check girl, Vicki, in her white riding breeches and black boots, coming across the bridge.

"Hello," she said. "Have you seen Mr. Cromwell anywhere?"

"Not this morning," I said.

"Where's Mrs. Bonner?"

"She's still asleep."

"Have you seen Kaye Gorman?"

"No," I said. "Isn't it rather early for any of these people? —It's just noon."

She pointed a red-tipped finger at me and nodded soberly.

"I think you've got something there," she said. She turned to say "Hi!" to a couple of men just getting in a car, and got in with them.

I crossed the street. A policeman, marking the front tires of cars along the curb with a piece of yellow chalk on a stick, had stopped at Judy's open cream-colored roadster and was giving her a third ticket.

"I'll get the keys and move this," I said. "It's owner's still asleep."

The cop grinned.

"The keys are in it," he said. "You can put it on the side street there. It'll be okay."

At three o'clock Judy was still asleep. The sun was streaming in through the long open windows. I drew the curtains and tip-toed out, hoping she'd sleep on. But she didn't. She woke up as I got to my door and sat up, looking around her, bewildered and slightly dazed.

"Gosh, I must have been asleep," she said. She rubbed her eyes like a flushed sleepy child. I nodded. She sat there, staring ahead of her, her eyes gradually changing as reality focussed in her mind.

Suddenly she raised her eyes to mine. A sharp spasm of pity tore my heart. It didn't seem possible that any twenty-one-year-old could hold such anguish.

"Call Clem for me—will you, Grace?" she said, unsteadily.

"You'd better do it yourself, darling," I said. "I did call him, and was told he didn't care to be disturbed."

She stared at me with parted lips and stricken eyes.

"Did you tell him who you were?"

I nodded. "But I'll call him again . . ."

"No, no!" she said quickly. "Never mind. It's all right."

She got up abruptly and stood by the window looking out. After a little she came back to the sofa, sat down and reached for a cigarette, and lighted it, without, I knew, the faintest awareness of what she was doing.

I picked up the phone. "Send Mrs. Bonner some coffee and bacon and eggs and toast immediately," I said.

She got up and went over to the window again. I could see her slim shoulders quivering, her brown fists clenched. Then suddenly she came back to me.

"Oh, I can't stand it, Grace!" she whispered. "I can't stand it! Oh, what have I done . . . what have I done!"

She let her head sink on my shoulder, her arms tightly around me, and mine around her. At first I thought she was crying, but she wasn't.

Then she galvanized into life at the jangle of the phone beside us. I looked at her sharply, completely dumbfounded at the change that came over her.

"Answer it, Grace," she whispered. "Please—answer it!"

I picked it up, said "Hello," and listened. I turned round to her.

"It's Joe, at the ranch," I said. "He wants to know if you're coming out."

She relaxed abruptly, and pushed her bright hair back from her forehead, pale even under its deep sun tan. God knows what she expected to hear. I had no idea . . . not then.

"Oh, yes!" she cried, almost hysterically. "Tell him of course I'm coming! Tell him I'll be right out!"

And she dashed for the bath.

Which is how I happened to be in my room half an hour later when Colonel Primrose—apparently free for a moment from Mrs. de Courcey—telephoned and asked me to go for a ride with him . . . and how, what with one thing and another, we were taking our horses out of the paddock, a little after six, and trotting around the race track, a mile or so out of town.

"Buck said he saw you," Colonel Primrose said.

We were going around the half-mile track, my horse, a two-year-old named Dragonfly, shying at every post.

"He doesn't approve of Reno. He thinks it's a cesspool of iniquity."

He cocked his head down, giving me an amused glance. He got a bullet in his neck at the Argonne, so that whenever he wants to turn his head he has to duck a little, which makes him look rather like a parrot. The impression is sustained by the way his dark eyes can contract and dilate, on occasion, with appalling shrewdness, behind the kindly twinkle that's ordinarily there. It's always there when he's talking about his Sergeant Buck, who was with him in the Army and now lives with him in the old yellow brick house in Georgetown lived in by generations of Primroses, and manages him as if he were the heavyweight champion instead of a retired gentleman of independent means who's turned a hobby into an amazingly lucrative profession.

"Well," I said, "he's finally discovered it's not me that's the triple threat, but Mrs. de Courcey."

I grabbed the martingale as Dragonfly shied at the grain in the center field, agitated by a sudden gust of wind sweeping across the flat.

"Mary de Courcey is a very amusing woman," Colonel Primrose said seriously. "She used to be a great beauty. I think she's still remarkably handsome."

"Oh, very," I said. "—If it weren't for her hair," I added . . . but not out loud.

Colonel Primrose glanced at me. "You've got a nice seat," he said.

We rode on. The sun dropped behind the bowl of dun-colored hills around us, a veil of purple and indigo and rose settled over them. The low grandstand with its banners and the neat rows of whitewashed stalls beyond the board fence might have been miles from Virginia Street and the Hotel Washoe.

"As a matter of fact," he said after a while, "I'm glad Buck's worried about Mary de Courcey."

"Why?"

He looked around at me with a chuckle.

"You've heard about red herrings."

"Are you sure it's she that's the red herring?" I asked, very stupidly.

We were going around the outside track then.

"I wish I thought it would make the least difference to you, my dear," he said quietly.

Dragonfly shied at a branch of cotton wood that the wind blew from one of the big trees lining the board fence along the back lane, and shied again at a couple of bluebottles buzzing around his ear. I was so occupied keeping him in order, trying not to let Colonel Primrose see that his sudden seriousness had definitely startled me, and trying to assure myself at the same time that it was just the old Army habit of being gallant to a lady, that I didn't notice the car parked by the fence where the track turns.

We cantered on in silence, past the old-fashioned hearse with its gold and black flambeaux and oval windows and black and gold fringed broadcloth fittings that had been abandoned there. Behind it was a couple of old carriages, abandoned like the hearse, and a sleigh with rusted runners. The door of the hearse creaked on its rusty hinges in the evening breeze.

I glanced at Colonel Primrose. He didn't seem to have noticed the hearse, which was odd, as he always notices everything. I thought for a moment that he might still be thinking of Mary de Courcey—or me. But I was quite wrong. He was looking back the way we'd come, frowning a little. He drew his horse up, abruptly.

"Let's go back this way, shall we?" he said.

He was curiously preoccupied, but I've long since learned quite unquestioning obedience when he suggests something. So I pulled Dragonfly around, and we cantered back the way we'd come. At the turn I pulled him down to a walk.

"These darn bluebottles!" I said.

Colonel Primrose was not interested in my problems. I doubted at first if he'd even heard me.

Then he said, "I noticed them," very absently; and added, "I'd like a look at that car."

We walked our horses over to it, Dragonfly protesting mildly, shaking his head, switching his tail.

And suddenly Colonel Primrose, a little ahead of me, said sharply, "Go back, Mrs. Latham! Here—take my horse. Go back to the fence."

I stared at him, caught the reins he tossed me as he dismounted, pulled Dragonfly around and got the two of them back across the track. I got off, tied them both to the fence, and ran back. It was then that I noticed for the first time that the car was a handsome green coupé, custom-built, with New York license plates.

Colonel Primrose was standing there motionless, staring into the window.

A bluebottle buzzed back, and away. I crept quietly up beside Colonel Primrose and looked inside. Lying slumped down on the yellow leather seat—with blood dried in solid streaks and still in viscid pools on the white rubber floor—was the body of a man. There was a ragged hole in the right side of his throat.

I knew who it was even before my horror-stricken eyes escaped to touch, even for an instant, the lean brown face and staring sightless eyes of Dexter Cromwell.

Even then they didn't rest there. They were riveted, as

Colonel Primrose's were, on the red-gold hairs caught under the man's hand clutching the tortoise-shell wheel in the steely grasp of death. . . .

6

I stood there, staring at the red-gold hairs, the universe swirling in a nauseating shambles round my head. I hardly realized that I was swirling myself until I put out my hand to steady my shaking knees and heard Colonel Primrose's voice —it might have been a hundred miles away—snap out at me: "Don't touch that car!"

He caught my hand.

"What *is* the matter, Mrs. Latham?"

"Nothing," I gasped. ("Oh, *don't* be a fool!" I told myself.) "It's just the . . . altitude," I said, more steadily . . . thus unconsciously bringing out the oldest of all Reno alibis.

I took a deep breath. "I'm all right now."

I looked at him, and tried to smile. He let go my wrist, but he kept on looking at me, his black eyes sharpened, and still a little puzzled.

"Do you know who it is?" he asked evenly.

I nodded.

"His name is Dexter Cromwell. I met him yesterday. My niece knows him quite well, I believe."

I added to myself: "You're not going to catch me, my friend." Those red-gold strands of hair under the fingers frozen in rigor mortis stood out in my mind like strands of the gallows rope. Invisible skywriting swirled through my brain: "Be careful! *Be careful!* Don't say too much—*don't say too little!*"

Colonel Primrose looked back through the window of the car.

"Take your horse, Mrs. Latham," he said shortly. "Go back to the corral. Tell the watchman, and phone the police. I'll stay here."

It didn't take me the fraction of an instant to think—and shake my head.

"You go," I said. "I'm afraid of that horse with my knees so shaky. Let me sit down a minute."

I pushed my hair off my damp forehead. "I must be getting soft," I added.

He nodded, and in a moment I heard his horse's hoofs

clop-clopping rapidly. I waited until I saw the dust rising beyond the far turn in the track. Then I took a deep breath,
tried desperately to control my hands, shaking with just plain
terror, and went round to the right side of the car. I didn't
want to dislodge his body, wedged under the wheel and
against the left door . . . not thinking, of course, that it
would take far greater strength than mine to move that frozen rigid form.

I turned the handle of the door, and opened it. The pool
of blood, dried on the white floor, was still viscid-moist where
it had seeped under the door. It oozed slowly down toward
the running board . . . the only live thing in that whole re-
volting place except the horrible buzzing bluebottles.

My stomach gave a dizzy crazy lurch. I wanted to slam the
door shut, closing back the oozing blood and the staring
dreadful eyes that kept watching me as if Dexter Cromwell,
Reno playboy, was not dead at all. Reaching out, I inadvert-
ently touched his hand. It was warm, outside, from the furnace heat that the sun, beating all day on the closed car, had
wrapped it in; but underneath it was cold with the profound
hideous cold of death.

I drew back and closed my eyes. Then I opened them
again. The red-gold hairs were still there, and they were
caught firmly; and I had to get them away. I mustn't break
them, and I mustn't release his hold, even if I could, for rigor
once broken would be too damning. I took off my clumsy
cape skin glove and took hold of the hairs again—pulling
cautiously at them, and so slowly, not daring to keep my eyes
long from the track behind me . . . sick with apprehension,
hearing all the time, as if it was beating an awful tattoo on my
inner ear: "Oh, I can't stand it, Grace—I can't stand it! What
have I done . . . what have I done!"

Nothing in the world could have kept me from getting
those silent witnesses out of the hands of Death. I pulled at
them, gently, again and again, and at last they cáme, and I
stood there with them in my hand, motionless and almost
sick with relief. Then behind me I heard the muffled rhythm
of hoofs. I thrust the hairs into the pocket of my blouse and
buttoned it with frantic fingers, grabbed my glove and closed
the door . . . Dexter Cromwell watching me, all the while,
with Lazarus eyes.

I couldn't tell whether it had taken me longer than it
seemed, or whether it had only seemed a century and Colonel
Primrose had been very quick. He galloped up, jumped off his
horse and had it tethered at the post beside Dragonfly before
I could recover myself and get my compact away again, with
the bright hairs in the bottom of my pocket under my hand-

kerchief, and tell myself I mustn't forget and pull it out till I could burn them in my room.

I went to meet him.

"The police will be right out," he said. He looked at me sharply. "You've got a streak of powder under your right eye."

I brushed it off quickly—too quickly, I realized, seeing the tiny smile flash in his eye and then fade abruptly. I followed him back to the car, my heart stone-cold inside me. I saw him stop at the door with a quick start, and stand—it seemed an eon in which worlds could rise and fall again—staring in through the window; and I knew, as well as I ever knew anything, that he had seen at once that the red-gold hairs were not there.

I steadied myself, waiting for him to turn around and fix me with those black sparkling X-ray eyes from which all the kindliness and humor would be gone, and all memory of friendship and the amused affection I knew he'd felt for me from time to time—ever since he'd first come to my house, the over-flow guest of a friend of mine at April Harbor. But he didn't turn. He simply stood there, until I wanted to scream. And suddenly behind us was the sound of a motorcycle, and then a car.

Colonel Primrose said quietly, without turning his head, "The head of the Department of Criminal Identification of the Reno Police is one of the best young men in the country."

I was still a little numb as I watched a lean-jawed, blue-eyed man, clean-shaven, with crisp curly blond hair, get out of the police car with the quick steel-trap spring of an athlete and with something of the determined air of a bulldog. He nodded to Colonel Primrose not only as if they'd known each other but as if they'd already met again a little time before.

"Stand back, you fellows," he said curtly. "Don't stampede here like a herd of buffaloes. Get out of those car tracks, Johnson."

I saw for the first time the tire tracks ending where Dex Cromwell's car had left the dusty road to come out onto the grass. The marks on the grass were gone.

Colonel Primrose moved aside to give him room at the window. He stood there an instant, looking coolly in, without comment. He turned back.

"The name's Dexter Cromwell?"

"Mrs. Latham identified him," Colonel Primrose said. "She met him yesterday.—This is Mr. Hogan . . . Mrs. Latham."

Bill Hogan, Chief of Reno's Department of Criminal Identification, detective, technician and—as I learned—widely regarded through these parts as the whitest guy that ever fingerprinted a prostitute or a cracksman, gave me a quick nod, and glanced at my jodhpurs and the two horses tethered to the fence.

"Yeh," he said. "I've seen him around the hot spots."

He turned to one of the men with him. "You go back, Slim. His name's Dexter Cromwell. You start checking on his friends—on the quiet. Start with the crowd at the River House and the Washoe. Don't let 'em know he's dead. Get his mail, and see if he had any phone calls today.—Was he staying at the Washoe?"

They all turned to me.

"I don't know," I said. "I met him in the bar there."

I watched the man called Slim start for his car. "I've got to get to Judy," I thought desperately, but I didn't dare ask to go in with him. Colonel Primrose would be waiting for me to do just that. So I stood there, watching the second police car back out and scoot off in a cloud of dust, helpless to warn her that the deluge was breaking and to get ready for it. I knew Colonel Primrose was watching me—even if his eyes weren't on me, as they weren't when I pulled myself sharply together and turned back to the car.

The doctor they'd brought joined them. They opened the door—the one by the wheel that I'd been afraid to open, and should have done, for Dex Cromwell's body was far too stiff to move and there was no telltale blood on that side.

"He's been dead for hours," Hogan said tersely. "Even in this heat . . ."

He put aside the cuff of the white wool jacket, blackened and stiff with blood, and looked at the square platinum watch on Dex Cromwell's wrist. "Stopped at three, but that's probably this afternoon."

He turned the stem once and nodded. "Just run down is all."

"I'll have to get him out before I can do much," the doctor said. I never heard his name, but I'm perfectly certain that the detective magazine, that later said he was a vet., Bill Hogan had picked up at a stable on his way out was either mistaken or lying. He seemed efficient enough, and he was right about the cause of death in spite of everything—or in spite of me at any rate.

"He was stabbed, with something pretty sharp and not very big," he said. "Not a knife. I can't be sure until I wash all this muck off."

"Sure it's not a bullet?" Hogan said.

"You can see it's not," Colonel Primrose said quietly, and with so much quite unconscious authority that they both looked round at him.

"The flesh sticks up round the edges of the wound—you can see something's been pulled out. A bullet at the point of egress would do something of the sort, but that's out of the question. There's too much blood down here—you can see it spurted out of the jugular. You're hunting a pointed weapon about a quarter of an inch square and as sharp as hell.—I opened that door, by the way. I'm afraid I forgot it wasn't my own case, for a moment."

Bill Hogan glanced at me, quite perfunctorily. I shivered.

"All right, boys," he said. "Let's get going. Hitch this light up to your battery, Johnson, and give me my camera. I want to get this fingerprinted before we take it in. You look around the grounds, Fred, and see if you see anything that looks like it could be used for a weapon. Make it snappy, boys—it's getting dark."

He turned to me.

"You'd better go back to town, miss. I can use the Colonel if you can make it alone."

"Surely," I said.

I started for my horse. Colonel Primrose followed me, and held him while I put my foot in the stirrup.

"I'm sorry!" I whispered.

I hadn't meant to say anything at all.

He didn't answer, but I thought his hand tightened just a little on my arm as he helped me up.

"Have the caretaker phone for a taxi," he said.

I gave Dragonfly his mouth, and he broke into a gallop. He couldn't get away from all that fast enough for me.

7

It was half-past seven when I got back to the Washoe. The doorman's hand was not half-way to the handle when I had the door open. "Pay him, please," I said, realizing I had no money with me.

I dashed through the door, and stopped abruptly just inside it. Sergeant Buck, in his circus outfit, was there in front of me, methodically putting quarters into one of the slot machines in the hotel lobby.

"Stop dashing about like a chicken with its head off!" I said to myself sharply, catching a startling glimpse of my face in the mirrored pillar behind the palms. It was just in time, for Buck turned around and gave me a fishily indifferent glance.

Then he gathered a large handful of quarters from the trough at the bottom and moved on to the next machine.

"Has Mrs. Bonner come back?" I asked the clerk at the desk as he turned to get my key.

"Not yet, Mrs. Latham."

I started to the elevator, and stopped half-way there. Mr. Hogan had told one of his men to get Dexter Cromwell's mail and check up on his messages. Perhaps, when they got to his friends . . . I turned back to the desk.

"I'll take Mrs. Bonner's mail up," I said.

"There's no mail, Mrs. Latham. But somebody's been trying to get her. A Mr. Charles Baker. He's checked out now, on the evening plane."

The clerk handed me a whole sheaf of telephone slips. I looked quickly at them. They began about two o'clock.

I looked up at him. "Mrs. Bonner was in till after three," I said.

"Yes, Mrs. Latham—but the maid said you didn't want her disturbed. And she hasn't been getting much sleep, you know!"

He smiled playfully.

"I didn't know," I said as coldly as I could. "And I didn't know you took your guests' problems as your own."

His face fell ludicrously.

"Why, Mrs. Latham, we only try to be helpful. Many of our guests—especially if they're socially prominent as Mrs. Bonner,—have to be protected from all sorts of . . . of intrusion. It's a recognized part of our service."

"Then I beg your pardon," I said.

"Certainly, Mrs. Latham," he said graciously. "We have many problems that the ordinary management of a first-class hotel doesn't have. We have to use considerable discretion in dealing with them."

"I'm sure you do," I said. I really didn't want to be outdone in suavity and worldly wisdom by a hotel clerk in a buckaroo outfit.

"And—if you'll pardon my mentioning it—you might suggest to Mrs. Bonner that she could be a leetle mite more careful with her car, Mrs. Latham. A man from police headquarters was in asking whether she kept it in a garage or parked it in the street all night. The police here are—well, nice, but nosey . . . ha, ha!"

"I'll tell her," I said—thinking that they were going to be a lot nosier before they were through. I went on to the elevator, dreadfully aware that the chase was on, and realizing fully that Judy's car was only a blind. Which shows how wrong one can be, no matter how many facts are staring her in the face.

I took a bath and changed my clothes. Then I went in Judy's rose and gray sitting room and turned on the lights. For a while I just sat there, and then I poured myself a drink of scotch and let it stand until the soda was flat while I paced the floor, wishing to Heaven Judy would come back. Wishing I'd never come to Reno . . . Wishing I'd used my head and opened the left door instead of the right. Wishing everything I could think of, except that I hadn't taken those damning red-gold hairs. I was glad I'd had sense enough to do that, no matter how badly I'd bungled the doing. I still hadn't destroyed them, it occurred to me abruptly—and also that I'd better do it at once.

I turned back from the open window where I'd come to rest for a moment in my pacing about, and started toward my door. As I reached it I heard a sound at Judy's door, and stopped, my heart almost bursting with relief. She'd come at last, then. I rushed madly across the room and flung the door open . . . and drew back. It wasn't Judy—it was the hat check girl from the River House.

"Oh!" I said. "Won't you come in?"

She came in. I knew by the strange guarded expression in her eyes that she knew something was wrong. Whether she knew what it was I didn't know. She came in quietly, took off her big white felt Stetson—autographed by everybody who's bought her a drink since the pre-Rodeo festivities had begun; it looked already like a page out of the phone book—and slung it on a chair.

"Where's Mrs. Bonner?" she asked, biting her full red lower lip thoughtfully and looking at me with narrowed lids.

"She went out riding, about three," I said. "With Joe, at some ranch. Where would it be?"

"With Joe? Bar B. W., then," she said slowly, still gnawing at her lip, tapping her booted toe on the floor.

"Do you want to call her?" I asked, seeing her eyes rest on the phone for an instant.

"She wouldn't be there now. Unless she and Joe . . . went a long way . . . or got lost."

She had a slow lazy way of speaking, as if nothing mattered very much, least of all time.

"Is there any danger of their getting lost?" I asked, rather perturbed.

She looked at me a long time.

"Joe's got a way of getting lost—if it's convenient," she answered coolly. A little smile—not a very pleasant little smile at that—creased the full petal-textured flesh at the corner of her ripe mouth into three provocative dimples.

"Meaning?" I asked.

"Oh, nothing."

She cracked her black crop smartly against her boot, and gave a short little laugh.

"Only—don't let Cowboy Joe's south'n drawl and open countenance fool you, Mrs. Latham."

She got up and walked aimlessly around the room, humming a tune.

"What are you trying to say, Miss . . . ?" I started.

"Vicki's the name," she put in for me. "Vicki Ray. The Ray's short for Eisenbeis, which is too hard for a girl to pack around with her. And would I like a drink? I sure would. This yours?"

She pointed to the glass on the chromium and rose bar.

I nodded. She took it in the bathroom and poured it down the drain, and came back, her nose wrinkled with distaste.

"There's something about a dead drink that gets me down," she said in her slow fashion. "I guess it's a complex. I don't like *anything* dead. I don't like to see these ring neck squirrels. You see them all over the road, coming home early in the morning. I guess the headlights blind them and they can't get out of the way. Or dead birds. I don't like to see dead birds."

She mixed herself a drink.

"I guess you think I'm goofy, talking about things being dead."

"Oh no, not at all," I said. "I don't like dead things either."

She sat down, spread her feet apart and sat bending over, her elbows on her white tight-breeched knees, her glass suspended between them in both hands, swishing the amber liquor around in it.

"Does Mrs. Bonner know Dex is dead?" she asked, without looking up; and added, "Officially, I mean?"

I suppose I'd been expecting something like it, because it didn't surprise me, somehow. It seemed a perfectly natural continuation of what she'd been saying.

"I don't know," I said. "Do you? Officially, I mean?"

She shook her head. Then she gave me a slow, startlingly authentic Mona Lisa smile, and said lazily, "Don't get me wrong. I know it because a friend of mine on the force called me up and told me to get under cover, if I needed to—hell'd be breaking loose before morning."

She drained her glass and got up. "I told him I didn't need to cover up—see?"

She poured another drink. I wouldn't have realized even

then that she was already pretty tight if she hadn't missed her glass with the syphon and sent a spray all over the rose linen curtains. She steadied herself and aimed better the second time.

Then she turned around and looked at me, not smiling this time. "I don't need to cover up—see?" she repeated. A belligerent note crept into her slow voice.

I nodded.

"I've got an alibi. I live at a boarding house in Mill Street." She sat down again.

"It sounds like Jane Austen," I observed.

She looked up. "Don't know her. Is she taking the cure?"

I shook my head. It didn't matter. The cure at Bath in 1805 wouldn't mean much to Vicki who'd taken the cure at Reno.

"Well, anyway," she said. "Your landlord keeps an eye on you, in boarding houses. He's your witness."

I suppose I looked puzzled. I felt so.

"You've got to have a witness when you get your decree, to swear you spent your six weeks in Reno, not in California," she said. "You've got to be here part of every day. Not that they all do it, but that's the law. Anyway, Mr. Tucker knows I came in early last night. He sits up till everybody's in, just like my mother always did. He's done it for years—Kaye says he did it when she stayed there. All bundled up in his overcoat in front of the kitchen fire. Last night he was waiting up for two girls who'd been up to Tahoe. They get their decrees tomorrow. I guess he doesn't want anything to go wrong, so they have to hold over a day. He'd got their room rented for tomorrow night."

That was pretty puzzling too. I didn't know then that if a "divorcée" is detained out of the state so that she misses a day or two in her six weeks' residence, she can make up her time at the end. It's important, because the whole theory of Nevada divorce is built on the idea that six weeks' continuous residence gives the state court valid jurisdiction in a case. They're strict about it, because it's the only thing that gives any pretense of genuine legality to the divorce mill.

"All I mean is, Mr. Tucker knows I was in last night," Vicki said. "So it just happens this is once it isn't me that has to cover up. It's . . . somebody else."

Her full red lips curved in a curious little smile.

"For instance?" I inquired.

"You'd be surprised," she drawled.

She looked a thousand miles past the polished toe of her boot.

"Well, they say blackmail's nice work if you can get it."

"And . . . can you?"

Her slow smile deepened.

"Wouldn't a lot of people like to know?"

She leaned forward.

"Has anybody ever told you a story, not mentioning names, but working out so you can put two and two together—"

She broke off abruptly, looking oddly at me again, and just sat there, staring at the floor:

"You don't seem to care a lot if Dex is dead," I said, after a while. It had been in my mind for some time, but I hadn't meant to say it. I was surprised hearing it come out.

Her face tightened.

"Sure, I care," she said. "But he's dead, so there's not much I can do about it, is there?"

She got up abruptly, went over to the table, picked up a cigarette and stood there a long time with it hanging unlighted out of the corner of her mouth.

"Why do you think I'm not over at that goddam joint checking hats?" she said quietly, without looking up. "Don't you suppose the minute Slim Maggio tells enough people confidentially to cover up, and it starts slopping over, everybody'll be on my neck trying to get the low down?"

Her voice rose hysterically.

"Do you think I want them all feeling sorry for me because he gave me the run-around? Don't you suppose I've got my pride, the same as Judy Bonner? I was crazy about him, sure—but that doesn't keep me from knowing he was nothing but a lousy, gold-digging bastard.—Oh, God, I wish I was dead!"

"Oh dear, oh dear, oh dear!" I thought. "How I wish Judy would come!"

I thought I really couldn't sit there quietly another minute. But I did. Vicki was pacing the floor, back and forth, looking like a lion tamer in a cage, thwacking her black bootleg with her crop, wailing over and over that she wished she was dead. I couldn't very well join her pacing, but I presently began to concur in her wish. "I can't," I thought, "stand this much longer without going mad."

And then came relief—or I mistakingly thought it was, not knowing Reno. Somebody knocked on the door. I called out, "Come in," and a girl I hadn't seen before walked in. She was well dressed, in ordinary street clothes, with a smart black silk crownless turban on her light hair, and a white tailored sports dress, and she carried a long green cigarette holder in her hand. She had a strange face, without animation of any kind.

"Where's Judy?" she asked dully, looking around the room.

"Out at the Bar B. W.," Vicki said.

"Oh."

The girl looked around again, and flopped down on the small of her back in a cushioned chair. She stuck her feet out in front of her.

"This is Mrs. Latham," Vicki said.

The girl nodded. She sat staring in front of her. Finally she said, "I wouldn't care if she just didn't read his letters in front of me every morning, and call him up when I'm taking a bath, so I have to hear everything she says to him. I don't mind the rest of it. But I don't think that's fair."

I glanced at Vicki. I had the curious feeling that it was visiting day at the lunatic asylum.

"Then what did you ever come out here with her in the first place for, you big klunk?" Vicki said.

She collapsed on her stomach on the sofa, rolling her head back and forth in the down cushions, trying, I knew, to ease the ache in her own foggy brain. It was the first I saw of the strange Reno phenomenon that no matter how miserable and unhappy anybody is, she can always take time out to listen to anybody else's woes, and genuinely too. I'm sure there's no other place in the world where there's so much disinterested emotion so freely given . . . or so much time wasted listening to broken tales of mismanaged lives.

"You might have known how it would be," Vicki said, without raising her head.

"I thought it wouldn't look so bad at home if everybody thought I was all for her marrying him," the girl said dully. "He works in a bank, and I didn't want anybody to think I was just being kicked out. He's swell, really. I didn't want it to be hard on him at the bank. And her husband's a nice guy too. He teaches in high school. He thought it would look better if we came out the same time—like nobody was getting hurt, just reshuffling the cards. And I don't care, really, I don't. It's just I wish she didn't read those long special delivery letters every morning while I'm trying to eat breakfast."

She continued staring ahead of her.

"No," Vicki said. "It's hard enough to get down anyway."

"I'm glad there weren't any kids," the girl said. She lighted another cigarette from the end of the one in her holder, and looked around at me.

"Have you got any children?"

"Two," I said.

"With the father, I suppose."

She got up.

"Well, tell Judy I want her to come to our party tomorrow. We go to court at eleven. You come too. I'm going to

get so drunk I won't wake up till after she's married him.—
Down in the bar, at half-past eleven," she added.

She picked up her purse.

"I'm glad Judy and Dex are going to get married the
same day she gets her decree. She won't have such an empty
feeling, still having a man's name and it not meaning anything. That'll seem funny. Well, good-bye. I'll see you tomorrow."

She wandered out.

"I wish Judy would come!" I said.

I got up abruptly and went to the window. The snivelling
tragedy of the girl who'd just strolled out, torturing herself
to save the faces of a wretched bank clerk and a high school
teacher in a small town somewhere back East seemed incredibly puny, and futile, and unreal, and brutal, as I raised
my eyes to the vast luminous star-studded night. Somewhere
out under it was Judy, bearing a heart-breaking burden,
worse than this one, and bearing it bravely. I opened my lips
to breathe some sort of anguished prayer for her. No prayer
came . . . only the old quatrain from Omar:

> Oh that inverted Bowl we call the sky,
> Whereunder, crawling, cooped, we live and die.
> Lift not your hands to it for help,
> For it as impotently rolls as you and I.

And just then there was a knock at the door. I turned back
into the room. Vicki had raised her head and shouted "Come
in!" And the door opened, and in came Colonel Primrose.

8

He looked at me, then at Vicki, and the most extraordinary
expression of relief came over his face. He rubbed his hands
together, smiling.

Vicki got up instantly and retrieved her white hat and riding crop. "I'll be going," she said airily. "See you later."

She turned at the door and gave Colonel Primrose a
slightly intoxicated smile, put on her hat, gave it a debonair
pat that I knew she was far from feeling, and sauntered out.

Colonel Primrose looked at me.

"That's Vicki," I said. "The hat check girl at the River
House."

"Oh," he said. His face clouded abruptly. "I thought it was your niece. I . . . also *hoped* it was."

For a moment I didn't understand. Then I thought of Vicki's full blue-black tresses, and came sharply back to the thing I'd wandered away from, listening to Vicki and the bank clerk's wife. My heart sank. Those bright hairs were still in the pocket of my riding shirt. I tried not to glance at my door.

I picked up a cigarette and lighted it, and sat down on the sofa to hide the fact that my knees were not steady.

"Well?" I asked.

He came over and stood in front of the sofa, looking down at me with troubled eyes.

"That's what *I* came to ask," he said.

"Really?"

He frowned impatiently.

"They've figured out that Cromwell was stabbed to death with a sharp instrument, early this morning," he said curtly. "They haven't found the weapon. But they've found out a good deal about Cromwell.—That he came to Reno with your niece, Mrs. Bonner, when she came out to get her divorce, for one thing."

I hadn't known that, but I didn't say so. I nodded, and said "So what?"

He looked at me soberly for a moment and went on.

"They have also learned that she was planning to marry him as soon as she got her decree."

I flicked my cigarette into the fireplace. "Clever of them," I said. "The papers have been full of it for days."

"Furthermore," he went on steadily, "that they've been quarrelling constantly—both in public and private—for a week. And that Mrs. Bonner was intensely jealous of his association with other women—with, I take it, considerable provocation."

He sat down beside me.

"Mrs. Latham," he said, "where is Mrs. Bonner?—I want to talk to her."

"I haven't the faintest idea, Colonel Primrose," I said, as casually and in as matter-of-fact tones as I could muster. "She went out riding at the Bar B. W. ranch as usual this afternoon, about three. I got in late, as you know, and I haven't seen her since I came. She probably went to dinner and to a movie, or dancing somewhere."

He looked over at me steadily for a moment or two. Then he leaned forward a little.

"Mrs. Latham," he said slowly, and very soberly, "you and I are old friends, aren't we?"

I nodded.

"Then—don't you know that if anything is disturbing you, you can count on me for help?"

"I'm sure of it, Colonel Primrose," I said. I hope it sounded as smooth and sincere to him as I thought it did. "But after all—you *are* a policeman, aren't you. And even Sergeant Buck—who is certainly your most devoted admirer —says you'd cheerfully hang your own grandmother. Not that *I'm* in immediate danger of being hanged, or anyone else I know. But, as you know, my niece was engaged to Cromwell—even if she still had a husband—and Mr. Cromwell is dead, and obviously murdered. And Judy's reputation"—or what's left of it, I amended to myself—"is very dear to me. Which is something that as a policeman you wouldn't understand."

He looked at me with some surprise.

"Except," he said, "that I'm not in this as a policeman— for two very good reasons. The first is that I'm a leading suspect—thanks to the fact that I opened the door of that car."

"I expect you'll be able to clear yourself," I said—very ungraciously considering it was my stupidity that had got him involved. He let it pass, with only a slight sardonic flicker in his eyes.

"The second is equally simple—in fact, it's my sole reason for coming to Reno. I don't expect you to understand it. But I do, however, ask you very earnestly to believe me when I tell you that all in the world I want to do now is save your niece from the consequences—if this happens to be one of them—of her own folly . . . and not get her deeper into something through any folly of yours."

I wasn't convinced. It was strange, too. A week before, I would have gone to him without hesitation, confident of his understanding and compassion. But not now. He was a policeman after all. Let him deny it as he would, he was still on the side of law and order. I was not. I was on the side of heartbreak, and folly, and despair. Let him hang his grandmother, I thought; I would do everything in my power to keep him from helping some politically ambitious district attorney to hang my niece . . . or put her, as they do in Nevada, under the lethal bell behind the gray walls of the penitentiary in the desert outside Carson City, to breathe cyanide gas until she was as dead as Dexter Cromwell.

But there was no use telling him that.

I said, as brightly as I could, "That's marvellous, then. You've taken a dreadful load off my mind, Colonel. I haven't seen her yet, of course, but I know she'll be horribly upset when she hears what's happened. And there's no telling what she'll do—she's completely undisciplined."

He looked at me for a moment, an odd expression in his eyes.

"Then suppose you give me those hairs," he said, pleasantly.

"Those . . . hairs?" I asked, as blankly as I could.

He got up abruptly, went to the window, and stood there looking out on the bizarre neon-lighted little city. Then he came back.

"Mrs. Latham, I always make a mistake about you," he said quietly. "I find myself thinking of you as an intelligent human being. But whenever we get in a tight spot, you invariably act in the most womanish way."

He was quite angry—and I'd never seen him angry before . . . not at me.

And I was angry too. "Then perhaps you'll be good enough to close the door quietly behind you," I said.

He gave me an amazed glare.

"I'm sorry!" he said shortly. "I'm staying, until your niece comes."

"In your capacity of old and devoted friend—or your capacity of policeman?" I inquired icily.

He chuckled suddenly.

"In both," he said—maddeningly calm again.

I got up and started toward my room.

"Then you won't mind if I go out, will you? I haven't had anything to eat since lunch."

He came a few steps after me.

"I'll be delighted to take you to dinner at the River House," he said. "You see, my dear, I don't intend for you to talk to Mrs. Bonner before I've talked to her."

"Then I'll stay here and quietly starve," I said. "You don't know my niece. I do. If we have to have a scene, I prefer to have it here."

"Then I'll order you some food from downstairs."

"You needn't bother," I said.

"You're being very foolish, Grace Latham."

"Only womanish, surely?"

He gave an annoyed snort, went over to the bar, poured himself a drink and swished the soda in it sharply. Then he turned back to me.

"Look here, Mrs. Latham," he began urgently—almost imploringly.

There was a tap at the door.

"Another demented customer for Judy's bar," I thought. I said "Come in."

A white capped-and-aproned maid put her head in, giggled

coyly and withdrew, obviously thinking she'd interrupted a tête-à-tête . . . although the atmosphere should have been tense enough to indicate its nature.

"Come in!" I said sharply.

She sidled in, blinking and scared.

"I just came to get Mrs. Bonner's laundry," she said. "I do it every week. I usually get it tomorrow, I mean Tuesday, but my mother's at the hospital and I won't be on tomorrow night, so I thought, if it was all right with Mrs. Bonner, I'd get it tonight. But I can make a special trip . . . I don't want to—"

"That's all right," I said. I hadn't meant to scare her out of her wits. "I'll get it for you. Where does she keep it?"

"In the hamper in the bathroom, ma'am."

I got up and went into the bathroom. The hamper was one of those combination bath seats and baskets, with a rose-and-gray chenille cover, a large "W" encircled in a wreath on it. I opened it and dipped in to pick up the heap of crumpled silk underthings in it. And I jerked my hand out instantly—something hard and sharp had stuck my finger so that it was simply spurting blood.

"Damn!" I said. It hurt like poison. I reached in again, more carefully this time, and brought up the whole pile of soiled clothes. Then I stopped dead, staring, pressing my body against the rose-enameled wash stand to keep from reeling drunkenly to the floor.

Partly covered with Judy's crumpled riding shirt was the miner's candle pick she'd bought in Virginia City the day before. The hook by the bobesh had stuck my finger, but it wasn't that I was staring at. It was the pointed shaft. It was covered with brown stain almost to the hilt. The shirt that it was wrapped in was stained with brown too. It was blood. I knew that instantly . . . and I knew whose blood it was. In my own hands I was holding the weapon that had slain Dexter Cromwell.

I don't know how long I stared at it. I only know that it seemed an age before I could tear my eyes away from it. In the mirrored wall in front of me I saw my own face, hardly recognizable, so contorted was it with horror and fright . . . and beyond it, behind me in the door, I saw Colonel Primrose, looking at the reflection of the awful thing in my hand. Then suddenly he was gone. I heard him saying, in a pleasantly matter-of-fact voice, "Mrs. Latham says you can get Mrs. Bonner's clothes on Wednesday. She isn't quite sure what's to go."

And I heard the maid saying, "Thank you—oh, *thank* you, sir!" I know he must have tipped her handsomely.

I sank down at the side of the tub, scarcely knowing it when he came back and took the candle holder out of my shaking hands. He wrapped it up in Judy's shirt again.

"Come along, my dear," he said. "Maybe we can talk sense now."

He closed the door behind me, and I sank down on the sofa and closed my eyes. I heard him, close beside me, pick up the phone and say "Get me Mr. Hogan at the police station."

I sprang to my feet and clutched his arm. "Oh, no, no!" I cried. "Oh, don't—please don't! I beg you, don't!"

He shook his head. Then he said, in an instant, "Hello, Bill. This is Primrose. I'm at the Washoe, Apartment 308. Can you come over? I've got the weapon that killed Cromwell."

It was just then that I heard a little choked gasp behind us, and turned to see Judy standing there in the door. How long she'd been there I don't know . . . her body braced against the frame, her knuckles white balls outlining the doorknob, her eyes great blank pools set in dark hollows, her mouth a scarlet slash in a putty-colored face. She was staring at the point of the candle holder sticking out of her stained blouse in Colonel Primrose's hands. Then suddenly, with an inarticulate and awful little cry, she pitched forward in a heap on the floor. Colonel Primrose did not move. He was gazing fixedly at the bright red-gold head on the floor.

I started forward, and stopped. In the door, looming massive and grotesque in his musical comedy clothes, was Sergeant Buck. Through a fissure in the congealed granite façade I saw a flicker of warmth and compassion as he bent down and picked Judy up as if she were thistledown. I stared dumbly, white-faced, from him to Colonel Primrose, still standing by the telephone. Buck's presence there, at that precise moment, told me what I should have noticed when I saw him in the lobby when I came back from the race track. Colonel Primrose was on the job—and he was on it as a policeman, not as a friend.

My hands as I put a pillow down for Judy's head were as cold and numb as her own.

And then, abruptly, as if he hadn't already definitely more than reason and sanity could endure, the door directly across the narrow corridor popped open, and out of it, yapping and barking, burst the two dachshunds, and behind them, scrabbling after their leash, came the flaming poll of their mistress.

She came to a full abrupt stop and stared in at us.

"What on earth is going on?" she cried. "John—don't tell me you're being totalitarian!"

She whirled on Colonel Primrose—I'd never heard anyone call him John before—and whirled round at me, and threw out her hands.

"My dear, it's the Army! They're all alike . . . it's like smallpox, they never get over it—or is it malaria you never get over? Well, it doesn't matter. Just *ignore* him—ignore him *completely*, my dear, it's the only way! It really is! It's the only way I ever got along with the General, insofar as I did get along!—Now let's all be calm and find out what's the matter!"

I wasn't calm. I was dazed. I simply stared at her. She'd abandoned her Indian maiden rôle and was stunningly gowned in a handsome black lace, high-necked dinner dress with a rope of pearls wound around the base of her throat. She had a lovely figure, and for the first time I saw her eyes, amazingly fine, with a merry hard-bitten light in them. I didn't doubt that she must have been completely irresistible when she was young, or wonder that men couldn't resist her even now. Even Sergeant Buck. I saw the ramrod in his back stiffen and his heels involuntarily come together.

She looked from one of us to the other, and down at Judy.

"Is it Cromwell?" she asked abruptly. Nobody answered —not that she gave anybody much of a chance.

"It's that row they had last night, John! It positively woke the dead, it positively did!"

Colonel Primrose's black eyes sharpened.

"Dexter Cromwell has been murdered, Mrs. de Courcey," I said sharply. I had to stop her, even if only for a moment, till I could recover my wits again.

Then a strange thing happened. For an instant Mrs. de Courcey's blue eyes met mine like the flick of foil on foil, and all her mannered loquacity vanished for a bare pin point of time. And in that flashing fraction of a moment I saw the truth . . . that she knew—knew already, had known before she even came into the room—that Dex Cromwell was dead. But I wouldn't have known it in another second, and nobody else would have.

"My dear—how awful!" she cried. "How simply awful! But I must say it doesn't really surprise me, not in the least. Does it you, really, John?—If you can quit being military long enough to admit humanity? You remember, in the Islands, at the Whites' that night?—But no; of course you don't . . . you couldn't possibly, you weren't there!"

She whirled back to me.

"My dear, now you must use your head, you really must— mustn't she, John? You mustn't say another word about their quarrel. *The police mustn't know!* I shan't say a word—wild horses shan't drag it out of me—and I'll speak to that terribly nice Mr. Ewing next door. He must have heard them too, he couldn't have helped it. I'll explain to him that he mustn't let on for a moment, that he—"

Colonel Primrose interrupted her amiably. "You'd better keep out of this, Mary." I think in spite of himself he was feeling a little sorry for me. But I was past caring. I bent down and touched Judy's cold forehead. Her long gold-tipped lashes moved against her bloodless cheek.

A sudden gust of cold air came in the open windows out of the night. I glanced up, thinking I'd better close them, and stopped. In the mirror above the rose-and-gray lacquer bar I saw Mrs. de Courcey. She was looking out of one corner of her eye at the gore-encrusted piece of iron wrapped in Judy's bloodstained shirt. And she wasn't saying a word.

Down the corridor I heard the elevator doors clash open, and the sound of heavy feet. I watched Colonel Primrose put his arm around Mary de Courcey's handsome shoulders, and propel her gently to the door.

"I'll see you later, my dear," he said softly.

She flashed him a pretty dazzling smile. I glanced at Sergeant Phineas T. Buck. He was fit to be tied.

9

I have a rather bewildered notion of what happened when Colonel Primrose closed the door on Mrs. de Courcey and came back into the room with Bill Hogan. I had a distinct feeling of relief that Hogan had come alone, not trailing clouds of official glory in the form of newshawks, photographers and confidential assistants who'd turn out to be confidential friends of every hat check girl, gambling house tout, bell boy and scandalmonger in Washoe Valley. Even then, I know I dreaded Judy's coming out of the blessed anesthesia of unconsciousness worse than anything in the world. What she might say, what she might do, I didn't dare try to think.

And then, as I looked down at her face, the suntanned skin unwarmed by the glow of blood under it, drawn in sculptured purity over the exquisitely delicate bony frame of her cheeks and chin and forehead, she stirred . . . and it all happened in quite the opposite way.

She sat up very quietly, completely detached and objective, almost as if her spirit had erected some sort of invisible wall about her, through which none of this could reach her. She looked at me, her yellow-brown eyes so expressionless that I thought for a moment she didn't know me. I had the crazy notion that she was suffering from concussion, or some sort of amnesia, until she reached out and took hold of my hand, softly, the way a small child does walking along a narrow difficult path.

It was Colonel Primrose who first noticed she was sitting up. I saw him looking at her, not directly but in the mirror, his eyes grave and searching. Her own eyes were fixed on the sharp pointed candle holder lying on her crumpled stained shirt. In their amber-flecked depths there was something I couldn't put a name to. It was a kind of subdued horror, too profound and moving to have any relation to fear . . . and yet I knew she was afraid, appallingly afraid. And yet the inner core of her was perfectly controlled. I could feel that in the grasp of her slim cold brown hand. It had held many a thoroughbred to jumps almost as high as the one she faced now, and with hazards of brush and ditch and pond almost as thoroughly concealed.

I think I must have taken a very obvious long-drawn sigh of relief, because I felt Colonel Primrose's sharp black eyes pounce on me like a live spark from an open fire, and then shift instantly to Judy.

"Do you recognize this, Mrs. Bonner?" he asked. His voice was quiet and reassuring. Nobody but Sergeant Buck and I would know it was a snare and a delusion. Buck cleared his throat. He might as well have warned a doe with a load of lead in its heart.

Judy's voice sounded a thousand light years away, I hadn't heard it for so long.

"Yes. It's my shirt, tailored for me by the Chinaman in Sierra Street. And it's my candle holder. I got in in Virginia City yesterday, at the museum and curio shop there. I know it's the same because of the old piece of candle in it."

"You know Dexter Cromwell is dead, don't you, Mrs. Bonner?" Hogan asked. He was struggling, I could see, between heart and duty—between treating her as a lady or a murderess.

"I know it—I heard it, this evening, at a bar in Carson City," Judy said. "And I heard that man say he was . . . killed . . . with that."

"—But you didn't kill him, did you, miss?"

We all started violently, even Colonel Primrose. Judy

looked up at Sergeant Buck, who had cast that minor thunderbolt, her jaw tightening, her eyes turning into little pools of brimstone.

"No!" she said. "But I—"

Sergeant Buck interposed instantly. "I wouldn't talk like that if I was you, miss," he said, harshly. And yet it had a tone of quite fatherly remonstrance—if anything coming out of one side of that grim mouth could properly be said to be paternal.

Judy looked at him, her red mouth going down dangerously at the corners. Colonel Primrose tapped the table, and Mr. Hogan looked surprised and definitely annoyed . . . and I, I'm afraid, looked not unlike the cat that had just swallowed the canary. Sergeant Buck and I were at long last allies. I didn't realize that we had been—in a sort of backhand alignment—since morning, before Judy ever entered the picture.

"How long have you known Mr. Cromwell, Mrs. Bonner?" Colonel Primrose asked.

"About a year," Judy said quietly.

"What can you tell us about him? We're simply trying to fill out a background for him—to find out, perhaps, who his enemies were."

Judy was silent a moment, her gaze shifting to a point on the rug by the fireplace.

"I met him at a cocktail party in New York, at some friends', and then a lot later. He came from Milwaukee—his father's a banker there. His mother died when he was sixteen and sort of . . . sort of threw him on his own—he didn't get along with his father."

"You came out here together?"

The color mounted in Judy's face.

"Not . . . exactly," she said, without shifting her gaze.

"What do you mean, 'not exactly,' Mrs. Bonner?" Hogan asked sharply. Colonel Primrose stood looking at her, pointedly not having asked the question himself, I thought.

Judy got abruptly to her feet . . . and as she did so, the cuff of her riding shirt caught on the twisted hook of the bloodstained candle pick, and sent it flying off the table, up into the air and onto the floor. It caught and stuck, its sharp pointed tip buried in the rug, a mute and ghastly reconstruction, in a sense, of the crime, and almost an accusation.

She recoiled a step against a chair and stood staring down at it, one hand against her open mouth, her face livid with horror.

"Judy!" I cried. "Stop it! Stop it!"

I caught her arm and pushed her down into the chair, and turned on Mr. Hogan.

"Are you trying to drive the girl crazy?" I demanded. "Can't you leave her until morning, or at least till her lawyer gets here?"

It was Colonel Primrose who spoke. "I think we can, Mrs. Latham."

Mr. Hogan bent down and pulled the candle pick out of the floor, covering it first with his handkerchief, and wrapped it in the stained riding shirt again. He looked grim and undecided as he glanced appraisingly at the shaking child in the chair, her hands covering her face. I had the sudden awful impression that up to that time he'd been wondering whether it was possible for anyone so fragile and delicate as Judy to drive a rude hand-wrought piece of iron into a man's throat . . . and that now he had no longer any doubt.

"I'll have to ask you not to let her go out again this evening, Mrs. Latham," he said. "Try to have her get some rest. Tomorrow'll be a hard day."

I locked the door when they'd gone and came back to the table. The sheaf of slips the desk clerk had given me were lying in a heap, pushed aside under an ash tray in the confusion. I picked them up, glad to have something off the subject but not as banal as the weather to talk about. I handed them to Judy, still dazed, slumped down in the chair where I'd pushed her.

"These are yours," I said.

She looked at them, dully at first. Then gradually she came to life, like a tulip bud opening out under the camera on the motion-picture screen. She made a sudden leap for the telephone, and stopped just as her hand touched it, her face and body completely transformed. She turned back to me slowly.

"If I phone, they'll be listening in, won't they?" she whispered urgently.

"I'm afraid they might," I said. "And furthermore the gentleman's gone. He checked out for the late afternoon plane."

She stared at me, her lips parting stupidly, her eyes going dull again. The sheaf of slips fluttered to the floor. She stood perfectly motionless for a long time, then raised one hand to her forehead and rubbed back her hair.

"I'd like to . . . be by myself a little while, Grace," she whispered, her voice scarcely audible. "But don't go very far away, will you?"

"No, darling," I answered. I went to my door and turned back.

"Judy—this is going to be in the papers in the morning,"

I said, in a matter-of-fact and practical fashion that I was far from feeling. "I'd like to cable your parents, just to reassure them. Do you mind?"

For a moment I thought she hadn't heard me. After a bit she gave me a baffling twisted little smile.

"I'm afraid you can't, Grace. Because there isn't . . . anything . . . anything reassuring to tell them."

"Okay, then," I said, trying desperately to sound casual. "I'll wait till there is."

I opened my door. "I'm going down to the bar to get a sandwich. I'll be back in ten minutes, if you want me."

She nodded. I closed the door behind me, reflecting suddenly that I was fast getting acclimated. I could hear the bell boy saying, "if you want Mrs. Latham just look in the bar."

10

The bar of the Hotel Washoe looked at the moment more like a morgue than a hot spot. The gaming tables were empty, the dealers clicking their chips and piles of silver dollars in vain. The bartenders in their white coats were in one dismal little huddle, the musicians in another. A few bewildered newcomers in Eastern clothes were in one corner with the hotel hostess, an Eastern girl in a red evening dress, treating them to their first—and last—drink on the house, and being determinedly and unconvincingly cheerful.

At the table at the end of the bar I saw Kaye Gorman, Whitey and Joe Lucas—Cowboy Joe—all more or less plastered, or pretending they were, with two other men and a couple of girls in Western clothes that I didn't know.

I signalled Eddie the waiter. "Get me a sandwich—anything but chicken salad—and a pot of coffee, over in a corner. I want to telephone."

He nodded.

"Are there any detectives in here now?"

He shook his head.

"Not unless it's that guy in the corner by the dollar machine," he whispered.

I glanced past him at the end of the line of slot machines —one-armed pickpockets, the bus boy at the Town House calls them—and saw, with a start, my admirer the dashing Mr. Steve Ewing. He was looking at me, smiling.

"I don't know for sure who he is," Eddie said.

I nodded. "Where's the phone?"

I know now, because a friend of mine who's a proprietor of a night club and gambling house told me, that phone booths and washrooms and cash desks are always placed so you have to pass the Scylla of the bar and the Charybdis of the gambling tables to get to them—in the hope that you can't withstand a dual assault on your lower nature. I never have to ask directions any more, but then I didn't know.

Eddie nodded toward the apex between the bar and the crap game, beside the musicians' dais, and I went along past the slowly whirling roulette wheel and the stacks of silver dollars at the twenty-one table, unconscious of both of them, and took down the phone in the booth. I was entirely absorbed in the necessity of talking to Clem Bonner. I hadn't dared phone from my own room. At a public phone the girl at the switchboard wouldn't recognize my voice, and I had Clem's number so I didn't have to use Judy's name for her to recognize.

I got long distance, and gave his number, Ashland 4-8180, and waited, listening to the fascinating relay race of voices gathering distance in to me as a fisherman gathers in his line, until I had New York and Clem's apartment in the narrow booth there in Reno . . . with the impassive presence of the butler blocking me again.

"Listen!" I said. "I've *got* to speak to Mr. Clem!" I didn't dare say Bonner. "Will you tell him it's his wife's aunt, Mrs. Latham, and I simply must speak to him. It's absolutely imperative!"

"I'm sorry, madam," the voice said. "Mr. Bonner has given orders that he is not to be disturbed by anyone whatsoever."

"Will you go and tell him what I'm saying to you?" I demanded, as urgently as I could. "Tell him that it's *terribly* important.—He's in, isn't he?"

I looked at my watch. It would be one o'clock in New York.

"Well, I presume so, madam." The reply was stiff and slightly pained. "He was a short time ago, at any rate."

"Then go and tell him at once," I said.

I could hear the door slam, and after an interminable time the butler's voice again, still more stiff and pained. "Mr. Bonner begs to be excused, madam. He does not wish to be involved in any controversy with any member of the family. Good-bye, madam."

I sat staring into the phone with a curious sense of receding space and hopelessness and defeat. Then I was simply angry. "Involved in a controversy" indeed, I thought furiously. I took down the phone again. But when the operator spoke I changed my mind and hung up again. There was no use phoning Judy's father. It would take him over a week to get to Reno, and there wasn't anything that I could say to him.

The phone clicked, and I took down the receiver. The operator said, "Shall I charge that call to your room, Mrs. Latham?"

"Yes," I said. I might have saved myself the trouble of coming down.

I went back into the bar. Eddie was putting a cloth on a little table in the corner. I sat down to wait for my sandwich. The table with Kaye Gorman and Whitey and Cowboy Joe and the rest of them was to my left at the end of the bar. I could hear Kaye Gorman's baby voice: "You'd better sober up, Whitey, you've got a long evening ahead of you," and his semi-belligerent reply, and I put my head in my hands, trying not to listen to their babble.

And suddenly it occurred to me . . . as a last resort . . . I got up and walked across to their table.

They all looked distinctly embarrassed and ill at ease. Whitey, who was as drunk as I've ever seen anybody still navigating under his own steam, tried to get up, and collapsed back in his chair.

"Hello, Miz' Latham," he said. "Told you was going to clear out of here, didn' I? Didn' I? Well, going do it. Going to clear out right now."

He made another attempt to get up.

"I'm through. You don' believe me, but I'm through."

"Sit down, Whitey," Kaye Gorman said.

"Aw right, I'll sit down. What'll you have drink, Miz' Latham?"

"Nothing, thanks," I said. "I just wanted to speak to you, Mrs. Gorman."

She looked at me.

"All right. Shoot."

"Privately?" I asked.

"Nothing private in Reno," Whitey mumbled. "Nothing sacred. Nothing holy. I'm going clear out right now."

Cowboy Joe grinned at me. "You better wait till the mo'nin', Whitey," he drawled.

Whitey picked up his glass. "Aw right. Clear out in the morning."

Kaye Gorman, still looking steadily at me, hesitated. Then she got up, and we moved to the corner of the bar. She stood, one foot on the rail, her elbow on the chromium edge, and said "Well?"

"I want Clem Bonner to know what's happened out here,"
I said.

The skin around her eyes contracted. She blew two long
thin ribbons of cigarette smoke through her nose.

"So what?" she asked.

"I can't get him on the phone," I said. "Will you call him,
and let me talk to him?"

She gave me a long minute's gaze through black lowered
lashes, her mouth twisting slowly into a cold and unbelievably
impersonal smile.

"The answer, Mrs. Latham," she said coolly, "is no."

She blew another stream of smoke past my face and said,
"I'm not interested in Judith Bonner. She made her bed, and
let her lie in it."

A slow familiar voice at my shoulder brought Kaye Gorman sharply around. "Oh, is that so!" it said.

My friend Vicki from the River House, less sober even
than when I'd seen her last, was standing there, steadying
herself on the arm of a new man.—It seemed to me I
never saw the same person twice in Reno.

"Well, listen, Kaye," she said. "That's the screwiest goddam advice you ever gave anybody, see? What'd she do if
she was a chambermaid? What would any of us do? There
wouldn't be any Reno if we started sleeping in our own
beds. There—"

Cowboy Joe came lounging over. "Shut up, Vicki,—you're
drunk," he said good-naturedly. He pushed her and her
friend along the bar. "Let's have a drink—on the house.
Eddie, what do you say?"

Kaye Gorman stood stock still, her face chalk-white, her
baby blue eyes blistering.

"Anyway—I'm not calling up Clem for your niece, Mrs.
Latham," she said, with suppressed venom. "I've had enough
of her—already. Let her call Clem herself, if she wants
him . . . or if she can get him."

She turned on her heel and went along the bar to Joe and
Vicki and the other man. "It's my turn to buy drinks," I
heard her say. "What'll it be, Vicki?"

"Scotch, if I don't have to lie in it," I heard Vicki say, with
her throaty rippling laugh.

I didn't hear any more. I went back to my table. It was
stupid of me, of course, to ask her, and still . . . I shrugged
my shoulders. It was a tactical error, I suppose. If you're taking another woman's husband, you don't want him helping
her—even out of murder.

After a little Eddie brought my sandwich. He put it down.
I nodded without speaking, and then, because he didn't go

away, I glanced up. He was looking down at me, his old-young face an almost ludicrous caricature of distress and sympathy.

"You don't honestly think she did it, Miz' Latham, do you?" he asked anxiously.

"Of course not, Eddie," I said. "Don't be ridiculous."

"That's what it looks like to me too," he said earnestly. "She couldn't of done it. Not as crazy about him as she was, and always kidding about the other girls falling for him."

He glanced furtively over his thin shoulder and bent down, pretending to be putting sugar in my coffee.

"It's Mrs. Gorman I'd put my money on," he whispered. "What's she out here for? She got her divorce. What's she come back for? Did you ever think of that?"

I put down my napkin and looked at him. He started nervously. "I don't mean I think she—" he stammered.

"Of course not," I said. "I just thought of something, that's all."

The bartender rapped on the bar just then, and he scurried off like a frightened rabbit. And I sat there, gazing absently at my sandwich, thinking. That "You don't honestly think she did it, Mrs. Latham?" kept reeling around in my head? Did I, or didn't I, I wondered? And what else could I think?

Her hairs clutched in his hand . . . the bloodstained weapon hidden, wrapped in her riding shirt, in her soiled clothes hamper . . . his philandering . . . their quarrel at three in the morning in her room—what else was there to think?

Eddie's "It's Mrs. Gorman I'd put my money on" would be the plainest kind of what they call wishful thinking. But I wasn't above it—not now when the idea was there, creeping insidiously in my mind. Why was she there? She had her divorce. She was a widow, and didn't need another. Clem was in New York, Dex Cromwell hadn't known she was coming. I was sure of that in spite of Judy's passionate accusation: "You just want to humiliate me—you knew she was coming!" But why had she come?

It was just hoping against hope for Judy. That's all I was doing, and I knew it.

I was aware then that somebody was standing beside my table there. I looked up. It was Mr. Steve Ewing, smiling his unpleasantly significant smile down at me.

"Do you mind?" he said, pulling up a chair, and before I could say "Yes, I do—intensely," he was in it . . . not across from me but at my left, his back to the room, leaning both elbows on the table in the most clubby fashion.

"You know, I owe you an apology. I thought you were a

divorcée, yesterday. But you aren't, you're a widow, aren't you?"

"You know," I said, "I would be awfully glad if you would go somewhere else. And if you don't, I'll have to."

The smile wiped off his face slowly, leaving it rather frightening, I was aware to my astonishment.

"I think you'll change your mind about that, Mrs. Latham, if you'll listen to me a minute," he said. He was looking at me with another smile then, a different one, and his eyes narrowed. I don't know how I knew it, because it was the first time I'd ever come up against it; but I did know that this was not funny, or . . . or the sort of thing that my kind of people knew about. It was low, and soulless—the sort of thing that goes on in slimy underground places where there's ignorance and filth, and where decent things aren't known. I was frightened—not for myself, but for Judy, slim and lovely and ignorant, too, in her own way . . . but ignorant of the things that this man knew, and that parts of Reno, and New York and Paris and the whole world, away from the other safe sheltered parts, knew.

"What is it?" I said quietly.

He smiled again.

"I thought you'd be sensible," he said.

I looked at my arms. I'd thought the gooseflesh must be visible all over them, but it wasn't—it was only on my heart.

"I do a little . . . amateur photography, from time to time, Mrs. Latham," he said slowly, looking straight into my eyes.

"Yes?" I said.

"I've got a negative that I'd be glad to sell . . . and considering the mistake I made yesterday, I'll sell it to you—cheap."

"What is it?" I asked.

He looked at me.

"You're being cagey, Mrs. Latham? In that case the price has gone up. Two thousand dollars. Do you want it?"

My hands were as cold as ice.

"I still have to know what it is," I said. "I might be interested."

"All right. You get out your money, I'll get out my picture."

"I haven't that much money with me," I said, forcing my voice to its normal pitch. "If I can see the picture, I can tell whether it's worth two thousand dollars, or . . . nothing. If it's worth that much, I'll give it to you at the desk."

He gave me a silky smile. "How do I know?"

"How do you know? You know that women out here haven't got any men they can ask to—"

"All right, Mrs. Latham—you don't need to say it." His eyes were pinpoints burning into mine. "Here's a print you might like to see.—I took it last night, two-fifty A.M., from Mrs. Bonner's balcony. I'll admit it's not quite what I was expecting to get."

He smiled offensively again. I felt the angry color rising in my face.

"But the police would like it . . . well, even better."

He handed it to me. I don't still know how I held it in my hands. My muscles were like water and my fingers so numb that I couldn't feel them touching the glossy paper. But my eyes, focussing blindly on the dim print, made out Judy's room, and Judy, unmistakable, standing straight and slim and taut at the table . . . and facing her, his hand on her wrist, Dexter Cromwell.

And then I stared at it. It wasn't Dex Cromwell—it wasn't! I stared blindly at it. It was some other man . . . and then I caught my breath. It was Clem Bonner, Judy's husband . . . Clem Bonner who was to marry Kaye Gorman, the woman who'd divorced him—and whom I'd been calling so desperately in New York!

Mr. Steve Ewing's voice insinuated itself through the confusion in my brain.

"Surprises you, Mrs. Latham?—It'll surprise the police too. Well, Mrs. Latham?"

I looked from the picture to him and back again.

"I can take it to the police, of course—or even to Mrs. Bonner."

I looked up just then, without reason or warning of any kind. Standing silently in back of Mr. Ewing, and looking down at him with an expression of quite unconcealed distaste, was a large and ridiculous figure in a buckaroo outfit. And Sergeant Phineas T. Buck's voice, like milk and honey to my ears, said, with ominous calm, "Something off color, ma'am?"

My knees shook so that I could hardly control them. I didn't know how long he'd been standing there. Mr. Steve Ewing, after one quick start, was looking at me, his eyes narrowed, his teeth bared just a little so the gold ones showed, grotesque but nauseatingly sinister.

"This is . . . Mr. Ewing, Sergeant," I managed to get out, trying desperately to sound natural and unperturbed. "He's a . . . a professional photographer. I'm just arranging for some pictures."

Mr. Ewing smiled a slow smile oily with triumph. Sergeant Buck smiled too, but there was no oil in it. "I get you, ma'am," he said, his brassy voice hideous with menace.

A hand roughly as large as a country ham descended slowly on Mr. Ewing's narrow shoulder.

"Then you can just leave me make the arrangements, ma'am. And you might like to burn that sample.—Come with me, Mister Ewing!"

11

Judy's lawyer Mr. Martin, of the firm Martin, Ellicott and Breckenridge (catering exclusively—and with the utmost discretion—to the élite of the divorce colony), was with her when I got back upstairs. I was still shaking from my encounter with Mr. Steve Ewing, and still dazed by the facts that his spying camera had disclosed . . . and still completely bewildered by them. What was Clem Bonner doing in Reno? Why hadn't Judy told me he was there? It was all totally incomprehensible—all except Kaye Gorman's coming out. The reason for that was clear enough, now. So was her intense, acidly-controlled outburst against Judy a few minutes before. So was the strange expression on her face when I asked her to call Clem in New York. That must have seemed very funny indeed, I thought as I shook hands with Mr. Martin.

I could see he'd just come, by the expression of unstartled professional amiability on his round face as he turned from me to Judy—like the headmaster making it appear to the visiting parent that her offspring is very happy, really, in spite of everything that's written home to the contrary—and patted her paternally on the shoulder.

"And *now* what's upset our little lady?" he asked, rather unctuously.

"Wait till you hear," I thought. It was plain, however, that it wasn't the first time Mr. Martin had been called in in the role of oil for the troubled waters. And I realized too, for the first but certainly not the last time, that a Reno lawyer is a sort of human pousse café, compounded of very neatly separated layers of lawyer, confessor, priest, psychiatrist, mother, father and friend—each layer in its own tongue the authentic Voice of Experience.

Our little lady stood looking dumbly at me. If only I could

know what was going on behind the numb anguished curtain of her eyes, I thought desperately, hoping she'd speak, hoping she had confidence enough in Mr. Martin to tell him what she couldn't tell me.

Mr. Martin frowned a little. He wore a bow tie, slightly artistic but not really flamboyant. Just enough to make him look—with his iron-gray hair cut a little long and a little Bryanic—the sort of older man that a lonesome unhappy child three thousand miles from home could safely confide in. The other members of his firm, I learned, looked like successful New York stock brokers, and were assigned to women somewhat older than Judy.

There was an Olympian quality to Mr. Martin's frown, and it was bestowed on me.

"You haven't come out, I trust, Mrs. Latham, to unsettle Judy's determination to go through with her action?"

I never, in the time I was in Reno, heard Mr. Martin, or any of his associates or colleagues, use the word "divorce."

"After all she's been through!" he added.

A note in his voice implied, with absolutely nothing he actually said to account for it, that Clem had made the poor girl's life an unmitigated hell and beaten her regularly every Saturday night.

"No," I said, acidly. "But Mr. Dexter Cromwell has been murdered—and as my niece seems bound to be involved, considering their friendship, we both thought she'd better have advice from you."

It would be incorrect to say that Mr. Martin was literally rocked back on his heels. But figuratively he certainly was.

"Has been . . . *what?*" he gasped.

"Murdered," I said.

Nobody at police headquarters, apparently, had felt it necessary to tell Mr. Martin to cover up.

"Why . . . that's incredible! Why, I just lunched with him yesterday . . ."

Mr. Martin came to an incredulous and bewildered pause. It's always seemed odd to me that when perfectly assured people like him become suddenly unassured, they take refuge in such meaningless things.

"I know," I said. "We dined with him last night. He's dead just the same."

He turned aghast to Judy.

"They don't say . . . ?"

"Not quite," I said. "They're going to shortly. Inasmuch as —for some totally inexplicable reason—the weapon he was killed with has been found in the dirty clothes basket in Judy's bathroom.—That's what we need you for."

Mr. Martin was a little pale, and more than a little upset. He wiped the perspiration off his forehead with an enormous white linen handkerchief.

"Well," he said. "I . . . I must admit this is a shock. Our business is confined almost exclusively to . . . domestic relations. This is most unusual."

"Well," I said, "it's unusual for Judy too."

He rallied hastily.

"Of course, Mrs. Latham. We certainly can take care of it—even if we have to retain outside counsel. Let me see."

He patted his brow again.

"Your course is to say absolutely nothing for the time being, Judy."

Judy looked at me, a little ghost of a smile lighting her autumny eyes.

"She's been very good at that so far," I said. "She may need you to see she still retains the privilege of saying nothing."

"No one is required by law to make statements incriminating to herself, Mrs. Latham."

"I know," I said. "The third degree has a good many possibilities. They don't necessarily have to use a rubber hose."

Mr. Martin's firm, I take it, knows little about the facts of life outside the marital relations. He was quite pained.

"You can leave that to me, Mrs. Latham."

"That's what I wanted to be sure of," I said.

He turned to Judy.

"You'd best make a clean breast of the whole business, Judy," he said. It was kindly but authoritative. He drew a chair up and sat down beside her. Judy got up instantly.

"There isn't anything to tell," she said evenly. "I didn't murder him. Why should I want to? I was going to marry him."

Except that she spoke quickly there was no sign of emotion in her voice. But there was a false quality in it. She wasn't telling Mr. Martin any more, apparently, than she'd been telling me. I got up, went over to her and put my hand on her shoulder.

"If Mr. Martin is going to help you, Judy, he's got to know something of the background of this business."

I took the snapshot Steve Ewing had given me out of my pocket.

"You might possibly be willing to show him this—or even want to."

She looked silently at it for an instant, her face freezing, eyes widening as the meaning of it struck her. Then she stood perfectly rigid, her mouth open, eyes dilated. She looked slowly from the photo to the window, back to the photo, then to me.

"Where . . . did you get this?" she whispered.

"From an admirer of mine," I said. "Another one is getting the negative . . . so you can have a lot of them for your friends' memory books."

I took a cigarette, struck a match, lighted the cigarette and held the match out to Judy. She looked at it a moment, then stuck the corner of the picture in it, and watched the flame crawl up and suddenly envelop it. She dropped it onto the hearth. The flame died down, the charred figures on the charred surface writhed convulsively and disappeared in a tiny plume of white smoke. I put my foot on them and ground them to ash . . . thinking all the while that if Buck gave the negative, if he did get it, to Colonel Primrose, this would be pretty pointless. But I knew it wasn't in another way—by the suddenly lessened tension in Judy's eyes. However useless in the final analysis, it had nevertheless for the moment made a bond between us that we hadn't had before.

She gave my hand a quick little squeeze, and turned to Mr. Martin, who was sitting there completely flabbergasted, like a rural audience at a sleight-of-hand performance.

"My aunt just wanted you to know the mess I'm in," she said steadily. "I'm tired now. Perhaps you can do something if . . . if they start to arrest me. I'd . . . I'd rather not go to the jail."

I looked flabbergasted myself. She was as cool and matter-of-fact as Kaye Gorman or Vicki Ray.

"And . . . I'll see you in the morning."

Mr. Martin hesitated, and bowed himself out. I waited till he'd closed the door and had time to get away from it.

"Well," I said, "there goes somebody else you've convinced you killed Dex Cromwell. If you really mean you don't want to go to jail, my lamb, you'd better start doing something about it."

She turned on me desperately.

"Where is that negative, Grace? You've got to get it, no matter how much it costs—do you hear me?"

She clutched my arm frantically.

"Look, Judy," I said practically, forcing myself at least to sound patient. "I tell you the negative is being got—far more effectively than you or I could do it, and that's that. Now sit down."

It occurred to me that I'd better close the windows. I went over to them and looked out on the balcony. Steve Ewing's camera must have rested there on the terra cotta balustrade. His balcony wasn't more than eight or nine feet

from Judy's. I looked to the other side. There was another
balcony—Mrs. de Courcey's, it would be. Between it and
Judy's was the fire escape, zigzagging up the side of the yellow fireproof brick building. I could see light shining out of
Mrs. de Courcey's window. Steve Ewing's was dark. I closed
the windows, drew the rose linen curtains, went back and
sat down beside Judy.

"A man named Steve Ewing took that picture," I said. "He
must have—"

Then I noticed her eyes changing, on guard again.

"Judy," I said, "—has he done this, or something, before?"

"I don't know," she whispered.

I took a deep breath instead of counting ten.

"Listen, Judy," I said. "This isn't getting anybody anywhere. Look—it doesn't make any difference to me what's
happened out here, not up to now. I hope you didn't murder
Dex Cromwell. But if you did, all the more reason for you
to snap out of it, and quit trying to conceal things that by
their very nature can't be concealed. If this Ewing has been
blackmailing you, say so."

"I suppose it was him," she said dully. "They say so many
things about Reno you can't believe."

She started to get up, but I pulled her back.

"Go on."

"Oh, I got a letter one day, stuck under my door. It said
something about a picture that I'd be interested in keeping
from my family, and they'd sell it for five hundred dollars. I
was to put the money on a certain table at the River House
at a certain time, and I'd find the picture and the negative
under my door when I came in."

"Did you—?"

"Of course not."

Her eyes flashed.

"Why should I? I hadn't done anything I was ashamed of.
I'd heard that's one of the things you have to be careful about
here. They're supposed to take your picture in gambling
places, or these . . . well, these places around here, and if
you don't buy them they're supposed to send them to your
husband. Then he can contest the divorce and get out of
alimony, or get custody of the children, because you're not
fit to have them. Or . . . or something. Well, I'm not getting alimony and there aren't any children, and anyway, I
don't do things I don't want anybody to know about . . .
and anyway, there's . . . there's nobody that cares what
I do . . ."

She was sitting bolt-upright, blinking her long lashes to
keep back the tears. I looked at her. "Judy," I said, "—is

that why Clem came out? Did somebody send him a picture?"

She nodded.

"What of?"

"Of me, and . . . Dex. He was just kissing me good-night. He'd kissed me good-night . . . oh, lots of times. But that . . . that wasn't the point."

She stared blindly ahead of her.

"What was the point?"

"Oh, nothing."

She shrugged hopelessly. "Just more of the mess that . . . that we made of our marriage. That's all. I don't want to talk about it. It was my fault—I don't blame Clem. I thought . . . well, I thought after she left him flat he'd got over being in love with her—but I guess it doesn't work that way. I guess it's true, the worse some women treat a man the more he's in love with them. I guess she's that type, and he is . . . and I'm not."

"Darling," I said. "If you would try to be coherent, and make just a *little* sense! What has that got to do with you and—"

"Well, I was his wife . . ."

"I know. I mean, if he wanted Kaye again—which seems pretty incredible to me, not being the type either—and you were out here getting a divorce so he can marry her, why should he object to a picture of Dex kissing you good-night? —Which is easily understandable, though best done out of the glare of the camera!"

"Well—he thinks I can't take care of myself, and—"

"And he's quite right," I observed.

She leaned her head back against the cushions and nestled wretchedly against my shoulder.

"I know I'm stupid, and . . . and difficult, but I was so . . . so crazy about him! I couldn't bear seeing him go back to her . . ."

"Of course you couldn't, and you smell exactly like a horse," I said, my face against her bright incriminating hair. My heart quailed again as I thought of that.

"I'm sorry," she said meekly. "I'll take a bath. But he hasn't got any right interfering with my life, even if . . . if it is a mess. It wasn't any of his affair if I was going to marry Dex."

"Was he making it his affair?"

She nodded.

"Where is he?" I asked.

"He's gone," she said in a dead little voice. "He doesn't want any scandal, with Kaye out here, and all."

"Where has he gone?"

"You said he went on the late plane."

"You mean this . . . ?"

I looked down at the raft of telephone slips of Mr. Charles Baker still scattered about on the floor. That had never occurred to me, even knowing as I did that one of the rules of criminals and other people who need immediate pseudonyms is to take names that begin with the letters of their real names. Furthermore Clem Bonner would have needed something to explain the "C. B." on his bags and linen.

The point, of course, was that he had been trying to call Judy from two o'clock on—and if he'd been trying to call her, then he hadn't been with Kaye Gorman. "Oh, dear!" I thought; "what a mess!" And now he was gone, probably convinced that Judy had given orders she wouldn't talk to him.

"He didn't like Dex," Judy was saying. "In New York they—"

A knock on the door interrupted that. I took another deep breath and said, "Come in!"

12

The door opened slowly. I had a sudden idea that everything had gone slow-motion—even from the tense waiting look in Judy's face as she watched the door, like waiting in the movies for the headless phantom to appear.

It appeared at last, but it wasn't headless. It was my friend Vicki Ray the hat check girl, and the reason she was moving slowly is that she couldn't possibly have done anything else and kept her superb and very formal balance.

She steadied herself against the door frame for an instant, closed the door with tremendous carefulness, and came in. She gave us a gallant little salute from the brim of her white hat and sat down so cautiously that she wouldn't have broken if she had been glass. Then she just sat there, looking at Judy, and Judy looking at her.

Neither of them spoke, but I knew they were communicating in some way. It was like watching a broadcast through the glass windows at Radio City without a radio hookup. I didn't, oddly enough, have any feeling that either of them wanted me to go, or that what they were thinking would ever be put in words even if I did go.

At last Vicki said, controlling her voice remarkably and

speaking even slower than she did when she was sober, "The cops are looking for a girl that a wop lives out by the race track saw running along the road a little after two this morning. He's sure of the time, because he's a waiter at a place in Center Street and he gets off at two. I understand he says he wouldn't recognize her, it was dark, but he knows it was a woman, he heard her footsteps.—So he didn't see her so much as hear her."

Judy didn't say anything.

"It's too bad Dex had so many women in his life," Vicki's voice went on, preternaturally slow. "A girl that works up at Tahoe says when he was here three years ago, getting his divorce, he used to throw parties up there that made even Reno rub its eyes."

Judy stiffened back against the sofa. "So what?" she asked, in a flat voice that I hardly recognized.

Vicki drew herself out of the chair onto her feet, and steadied herself against the table.

"If we could show he knew dope peddlers enough, and shills, and marathon dancers, and divorcées hiding out in tourist camps that call themselves guest ranches, well . . ."

She started toward the door. "Well, I'm just interested, that's all."

She got to the door and outside, and closed it carefully.

I looked at Judy. Her slim body had relaxed, her eyes were closed, her brown little hands lay listlessly in her lap.

The door opened again, very slowly, and Vicki's head came slowly back.

"Say—who's the guy Baker that Kaye Gorman drove out to the airport in Whitey's car this afternoon?"

I didn't look at Judy, but I could feel her stiffen again with the suddenness of an electric shock.

"I don't know—why?" she said sharply.

"I thought you did—the telephone girl said he'd been calling you all day. She figured he's somebody that knew you."

She closed the door again. Judy got up slowly and picked up the sheaf of telephone slips, and tore them up, slowly, into a thousand pieces, and let them slip through her fingers into the waste basket. Then she turned around and gave me a twisted little smile. "Well," she said, "that's that. And Judy's going to bed."

I went to my door. I didn't kiss her good-night. I couldn't have, possibly. She had erected an invisible but perfectly impenetrable wall about herself that excluded any softness or sympathy.

At the door I turned.

"Judy," I said. "I don't believe you killed Dexter Cromwell.

But there's a lot of evidence that's very damning indeed. And I dare say I'm being pretty stuffy and old-fashioned . . . but I would like to hear you say you didn't do it—with your own lips."

She looked at me very steadily for a moment. Then she said, "Would you believe it if I did?"

"Would I?" I thought desperately. I think she saw the stab of doubt in my eyes, because she smiled faintly.

"You don't have to, darling. because I haven't said it—have I?"

"No," I said.

"No," she repeated softly. And she added, after a moment, "and I'm not going to—not to you."

She stood there, erect and young and very lovely, more like a Jeanne d'Arc than a . . . I tried to think of the name of a woman who had murdered her lover, but my brain was foggy and numb. So I said, "Good night, Judy," went into my room and closed the door.

I went to the window without turning on the light, and stood there looking down on a paved patio where a lighted fountain played over potted ferns in a pool. The patio was empty. Music from the bar came faintly through the closed French windows. I was thinking of Judy . . . and I was aware now for the first time that I didn't really, in my heart, believe she had killed Dex Cromwell. I tried to analyze that feeling, but I couldn't. It wasn't reasonable. Reason was all against it—reason, and evidence. The gold hairs clutched in his dead hand, the miner's candle pick, the shaft covered with blood, in her clothes hamper, were objective and irrefutable. She had been there, on the race track, near him, when he died. The weapon that had killed him was hers. She had bought it the day before. It was in her room . . . in a place that would not be disturbed until the next day, and that actually had been disturbed sooner only by the accident of the night maid's mother being ill.

Then there was all the rest of it. Her jealousy of Kaye Gorman, her wild quarrel with the husband she was divorcing, just before it all happened. And the thing I'd been trying to avoid thinking about all day and had to face at last: the long, long sleep that had followed all this, as if some tremendous emotional crisis had been reached, and Judy, who hadn't slept apparently for days, had slept, without taking off her clothes or getting into bed.

While I stood there looking down into the court, this conviction of mine gathering coherence, I saw the door of the bar open and a couple come out. Even in the half-light of the orange flambeaux against the walls I recognized the white head and spindly legs of one of them, and in another moment I saw the glint of the red hair of the woman with him. They strolled to the far end of the patio and stopped. Whitey looked up at the windows, mostly dark now except for those along the corridor, on the side opposite me.

Then a rather strange thing happened. Mrs. de Courcey opened her bag and handed him what was evidently a roll of bills, for he counted them off rapidly before putting them in his pocket. Then, almost instantly, he crossed the patio again and disappeared into the bar.

Mrs. de Courcey stood under the potted palms a little while, lighted a cigarette, flicked the match into the pool under the fountain and sat down in one of the white-and-yellow chromium-armed sofas, her elegant black figure outlined against the light ground. From time to time she bent forward and glanced at the door to the bar. She must be waiting for Whitey to come back, I thought, though what he'd be likely to be getting with that much money I could only make the most lurid guesses at.

I stood there, spying on her, I suppose, just as Steve Ewing's camera had spied on Judy and Clem Bonner. I didn't think of it as that. Being a natural-born busybody, it never occurred to me, somehow, to go away from the window and turn on my light and mind my own very upsetting affairs.

Mrs. de Courcey stood up, and moved forward, her hands outstretched—not to Whitey bringing her any of the things I'd thought of, but to a man coming from the lobby side of the patio. They met by the fountain. For a moment I thought she was going to kiss him . . . and then there was the bang of a door and a stentorian throat-clearing.

The man turned quickly. I didn't need to see Sergeant Buck's large and fantastic form come forward. I already knew it was Colonel Primrose that Mrs. de Courcey had been waiting for in the patio, and that Sergeant Buck was there on the job in his self-appointed role of duenna.

I pulled down my shade—wondering a little if this was another red herring—and turned around. My travelling clock on the table said quarter to one. Somehow the idea that it was really quarter to one, and hence time to go to bed, never entered my mind. Like the fancy dress for the Fourth of July Rodeo, and the divorce parties, and gardenias, and slot machines in the grocery stores, it was just part of Reno. I haven't a doubt there are large numbers of people there who go to bed and sleep like Christians—even divorcées, I suppose— but they just happened to be people whom if I met at all I never knew personally. Everybody I knew—except Mr. Tucker, whom I hadn't at this point met—could be found at any time of the early morning somewhere in the district bounded by Lake Tahoe and Carson City on the one hand and Pyramid Lake and Virginia City on the other, with Reno lying neatly in the center. And it was usually easy to say just where, when you knew them, which I didn't, not then.

I got out a jacket and was just turning out my light when the door opened and Judy came in. She was still dressed. I began to wonder if I'd ever see her in anything but those wrinkled jodhpurs and scuffed jodhpur boots and crumpled shirt on which the tears had dried in spots. She was pale and there were big circles under her eyes, and under the remnants of her scarlet lipstick her lips were bloodless.

"I know you want to go to bed, Grace," she said wanly. "But would you—if you don't mind—put this in the mail box for me . . . outside the hotel? I'm afraid to put it in the chute."

She held out a stamped envelope.

"You see, Grace—nobody must know Clem was here. It's terribly important!"

I took the letter and put it in my pocket, not really understanding.

"Kaye Gorman knows he was here—that's somebody already," I said.

She gave a strange little laugh. "She won't tell."

"I hope you're right," I said.

"I know I am. But you'll do that, won't you?"

"Surely."

She turned back to the door, and stopped again. "You'll forgive me, Grace, won't you, being so . . . so difficult. That's what Dad calls it when I'm being completely foul. But you see—it's not just . . ."

"Listen, darling," I interrupted. "You're being very sweet, and I'm very fond of you. And if there are things you want to keep to yourself, do it and don't worry about me. But don't make yourself any unhappier than you have to . . . and go take off those clothes and take a bath and go to bed. Okay?"

She looked at me a moment or two and nodded. "Okay," she whispered.

I closed my door and locked it and started down the hall. As I did, a man who had obviously just stepped out into the corridor, as he wasn't there before I'd turned around to lock my door, stepped back into the maids' supply room and pulled the door to. My heart sank with a cold plop. I don't know why it hadn't occurred to me that the police would of course be watching her, and that while she might not be technically under arrest, practically she had to be, since that blood-stained weapon had been found in her possession.

For a moment I started to go back and stay with her. Then I decided it would be better if I didn't. I've always thought it must be very difficult for a doomed man having somebody, even—or especially—his spiritual adviser, with him to the end. And the policeman there in the maids' cubby hole cast a shadow of doom over Judy Bonner that all my conviction of her essential innocence could not quite dispel. Nevertheless I nodded to him when he peered out, to show him I knew he was there and why, and perhaps from the primitive belief that if you speak to the devil when you meet him you exorcise him. I've often wondered if that's why colored people in country lanes always speak to strangers.

This man was neither the devil nor strange—I'd seen him already at the race track. Nevertheless, and not entirely without guile, I said to him, "You'll see that no one disturbs my niece while I'm out, won't you? She's trying to get some rest."

Which, like practically everything else I did in Reno, shows with a brilliant clarity the essential wisdom of minding one's own business, or possibly just letting well enough alone.

"Sure, I'll take care of her, Mrs. Latham—don't you worry. You'll be in the bar, I guess, if anybody wants you?" he added innocently.

"That's right," I said. "Either a bar," I added to myself, "or a gambling hell, or just roaming the streets."

There weren't many people in the lobby as I went through —a man in cowboy clothes playing blackjack with the night desk clerk, a little crowd of people all more or less sober standing around talking.

I went out into the brilliantly lighted street. It was cool and quiet. Across the street the big sign of the Riverside Hotel did its maddening routine of white, pink, blue and back again, over and over. I started across the bridge, thinking I'd better not go to the post office directly for fear they were watching me too. Halfway across I heard footsteps and looked back. Sergeant Buck was coming after me in his familiar double-quick, so I waited. He came to a smart halt, and while he didn't actually salute, I had the impression of being pretty military myself and rather receiving intelligence in line of battle.

"I attended to that matter of the picture, ma'am," he said.

I said, "Thank you—so much! Where is it?"

"It got accidentally burned up," he answered, and spat neatly down into the Truckee.

"That's too bad," I said.

"Yes, ma'am," he answered with a certain sinister relish. "Irregardless of the fact it wasn't of her in what you'd call an uncompromising position exactly, it don't hurt to pin the ears back on those babies."

Not knowing who the man in the picture was, Sergeant Buck could not possibly know just how uncompromising— in a very literal sense—that picture had been. I wondered for a moment if I should tell him, and thought not.

"I'll be getting back now, ma'am," Sergeant Buck said. "And I wouldn't go traipsing around the streets alone, if I was you. It ain't safe, and it ain't ladylike."

Which in Reno is wrong. A lone woman in the streets and in night clubs and gambling joints is safer, I should think, than she might be alone in her own apartment in New York. Physically safer . . . and the moral danger she runs, in the line of how much she drinks and gambles, is entirely up to her. And the unique conventions of a place where there are so many lone women make it perfectly ladylike for her to go anywhere by herself. It may not be fun, but it's correct. And ordinarily she doesn't stay alone more than a moment or two. As I discovered practically immediately.

13

I posted Judy's letter in the mail box on the corner of Virginia Street. The neon-lighted oasis of the River House reminded me of the sandwich I'd left untouched on the table after my encounter with Mr. Ewing, and I turned along First Street and went in. A crowd of people in varying degrees of Westernalia were dancing to the aching moan of a cowboy orchestra from Hollywood. Half a dozen little groups were seated on high leather-topped stools at the bar. The news of Dex Cromwell's murder had spread to all the regular customers. Everybody—even the dealers in a little huddle at the end of the deserted row of brightly lighted gambling tables—was discussing it . . . in discreet guarded undertones, so that the dancers, who were mostly transient visitors, neither members of the divorce colony nor the town, weren't aware that anything out of the ordinary had happened. It is part of the code of Reno to protect its visitors from open gossip and unfavorable publicity. There's a constant underground struggle that goes on between the people who profit by keeping Reno's veneer of respectability polished and intact, and the Steve Ewings's and newspaper gossip writers snooping about for a juicy paragraph for the outside world to read for breakfast and say with the Pharisee, "I am not as other men."

As I came in someone looked around, and there was a little hush. Frenchy, the proprietor, came forward and greeted me, and Whitey disengaged himself from a little group at the end of the bar and came forward too.

"I'd like something to eat," I said.

Whitey, oddly enough considering the apparent state he'd been in at the Washoe Bar, was quite sober.

"Can I sit with you?" he asked. If I hadn't just happened to notice the little sign he gave one of the men at the bar I should have thought nothing but the finest motives of sympathy and friendship motivated him—until I got my bill for his supper that he didn't eat and his wine that he didn't drink and a good deal of rye that he did.

"Listen, Whitey," I said, when I'd ordered. "How long have you known Dex Cromwell?"

His white eyelashes blinked rapidly. I didn't realize that according to the Reno code I shouldn't have come right out with such a question at such a time. He wrinkled his sunburned brow.

"Gee, now, Miz' Latham, let' see. I guess quite some time," he said. "First time was in L. A. when I was working in the movies, about ten years ago. Then I come up here when he was getting his divorce, about three years ago."

"Did you know Mrs. Gorman then too?"

"Sure, I knew Kaye. Kaye's a real lady."

"And Vicki—I mean was she here?"

"Jeez, no, Miz' Latham—Vicki wasn't here then."

"But she knew Dex before he came out this time, didn't she?"

"I don't think so. But don't pay no attention to Vicki, Miz' Latham—she's nuttier'n a fruit cake."

At that moment Vicki came in from the other room, behind her Kaye Gorman and Joe Lucas, his two big hands on her shoulders, pushing her inside. He saw me first and gave me a broad good-natured grin. Kaye Gorman, who seemed intensely aware of everything he did, followed his eye quickly. Her baby face tightened, then she smiled politely—as she would have done in the East—and twisted her shoulder to shake Joe's hands off.

"If that ain't the payoff!" Whitey muttered angrily. "The son of a buck!"

"What's the matter?" I asked.

"Look at that dirty chisellin' rat!"

He pushed his chair back with a restrained violence and got up, muttering and mumbling. "I'm going to clear out of here, Miz' Latham. If she wants to be seen playin' around that . . ."

He was gone. But before Kaye Gorman and Joe got to the table—Vicki had disappeared somewhere—he was back, retrieved his glass and was gone again.

"Hello, Miz' Latham," Joe drawled, with his slow soft voice and open engaging grin. "How's Mis' Judy? Ah hope she ain't lettin' this upset her none."

"Oh, shut up, Joe!" Kaye said angrily. "Lay off this 'ain't' and 'none'. Anybody'd think you *were* a cowboy."

She sat down.

"You know it burns me up. You wouldn't think he'd been to college, and could talk like a civilized Christian if he wanted to. All this lingo that pulls 'em in just gives me a pain. Just cut it out when you're around me. And go on and get a drink—I want to talk to Mrs. Latham."

Joe winked at me and grinned. "Okay, sugah," he drawled.

Kaye Gorman flushed angrily. She was in a filthy mood. Cowboy Joe grinned again and ambled away, and in a minute was dancing with a pretty little dark-haired, madonna-eyed girl who couldn't have been more than a child and came to about the middle button of his plaid shirt.

"She's a sweet thing," I said to Kaye Gorman. She had been staring moodily down at the table.

"I'll say," she said. The soft peachblossom skin around her hard blue eyes twitched. "She's twenty-two. This is her third trip out. She started with an eighteen-dollar-a-week clerk in a brokerage office, and she's worked up to the senior partner's son."

"More power to her," I said.

She laughed her short laugh.

"I guess you think I'm a hot one to be talking."

"Something of the sort," I answered. I was thinking, "And this is the woman Judy let take her husband away from her." It didn't make sense—not until I really looked at her. Joe and the little madonna-eyed girl danced by. Kaye looked up at him, her baby blue eyes blank and ingenuous, her round baby face as guileless as a kitten's, smiling. He gave the girl in his arms a playful squeeze and winked at Kaye as if to tell her it was intended for her, and danced on. A little smile dimpled in the corners of her red cupid's-bow mouth, and faded as he went out of sight. She sort of shook herself, and came back to me.

"I'm sorry if I was rude to-night," she said abruptly. "But I thought you were . . . either kidding me, or . . . oh, well, trying to stick something on me."

"No," I said. "I just didn't know he'd been here. I take it it's being kept a secret."

She ground out the cigarette she'd just lighted in Whitey's bread and butter plate. The hot ash touched the butter and smouldered noxiously. Her face was a curious study in bitterness, and something else I couldn't name.

"I'm not trying to keep it a secret, if that's what you mean," she said without looking up.

I was rather taken aback by that, remembering Judy's calm assurance.

"Listen, Mrs. Latham. It doesn't matter to me how much mud the inkslingers plaster on your niece. I told you that, and there's nothing personal intended. But if Clem wants to be so careful to protect her name, and all the rest of it, what did he have to come out here for in the first place? It's all a lot of baloney, if you want my opinion. You could have knocked me over with a feather when I saw him come sneaking up the back stairs last night. I thought I was going crazy."

I looked at her incredulously.

"Do you mean you didn't know he was out here?" I asked, trying not to sound too bewildered.

She pushed her chair back and faced me with her baby eyes full of cold contempt.

"Don't tell me you've fallen for that too? Say, Mrs. Latham, do I look like a fool?"

I was so completely at sea in this sudden whirlpool of contradiction that I just shrugged my shoulders and went on eating, hoping if I didn't say anything it would clear up in some miraculous fashion.

"Well, I'm not—not quite," she said, in her hard flat voice. "You just said more power to that gal out there. Well, that's what I say when I'm not pretending I'm shocked. I was poor when I was a kid. I didn't have anything but my face to go on, if you call it my face, and I wasn't going to work my head off like my sister—working in offices, marrying a fellow not getting much more than she was, having a batch of kids, working like a dog . . . Not me. She says she's happier than I've ever been, but you can't fool me. She hasn't had but one new dress since they started buying the house, and the poor sap she married goes without lunch to buy her a dozen tulip bulbs for the garden, and the kids have to sell magazines after school to buy a punching bag, and a projector for the movie camera they bought running errands for the grocer."

I smiled. Without knowing it Kaye Gorman had described a happy family.

"Well, not me. I married Clem not because I fell in love with him but because I wanted money and his family had it. It wasn't my fault they lost it, and Clem was just as glad to get rid of me as I was of him. His mother stuck by his father, but that wasn't the same. She didn't care if she had to wash the dishes—she hadn't been doing it all her life. Well, Mr. Gorman wasn't much on looks, maybe, and he was a lot older than me. But he had money."

I looked at her. Her eyes were bright and her cheeks flushed.

"But that's not the point. The point is, I got what I went after. Nobody's going to take it away from me, and . . . now it's going to get me the other things I want.—And Clem Bonner doesn't happen to be it."

"You mean," I began slowly . . .

"I mean I wouldn't marry Clem Bonner again to save my neck," she said curtly.

Then she laughed. She knew what I was thinking almost before I knew it myself.

"Nor Dex Cromwell either. He and I were in the same business . . . only I got where I was going and he got it in the neck first."

I shuddered, still seeing that slumped figure with the wound in his throat. Kaye Gorman didn't know how literally she was speaking.

"He's been laying for somebody like Judy a long, long time. His first wife was just a leg up the ladder, the poor sucker. She was crazy about him. He stuck by her just long enough to salt away a few nuts for the long winter before somebody like Judy fell for him."

The waiter stopped significantly by her chair. She shook her head. "I'm on the wagon, Jean." She laughed a little as he moved away.

"I've been on the wagon ever since I had a look at what it's doing to Vicki."

"Have you known Vicki before?"

She looked at me quickly.

"No," she said laconically. She was rolling bits of bread between her red-tipped fingers.

"Have they found out who shot Dex?" she asked abruptly. Her eyes widened, ingenuous but not enough so to hide the steady wary gleam back behind them.

The finding of the candle pick in Judy's bathroom apparently had not spread as far as her ears yet.

I shook my head. "He wasn't shot. He was stabbed."

"Oh, God, how awful," she said. "He . . . hated messy things so."

She stared moodily down at the table again. I looked at her for several moments. Was she telling me the truth about Clem Bonner, I wondered? I believed what she said about Cromwell, somehow. There wasn't anything he could give her. The giving would have been on her side. And I don't think she ever gave. She took. But Clem was different. He had social position, for one thing, that her money alone wouldn't ever give her. And there must have been some reason for everybody—from Judy to the gossip writers—thinking what they did. And if she was telling the truth, and she didn't want Clem or Dex, why had she come to Reno? But the moment when I could have asked her was gone.

So I said, "How long are you staying?"

"A couple of weeks."

I said, "Oh."

"Well," she said, "why don't you say it?"

There was a rudeness in her voice that I doubt if she meant entirely.

"Say what?" I asked.

"What am I doing in Reno. That's what you're thinking, isn't it?"

"Yes," I said. "It is. But I thought it wasn't any of my business, since it's not concerned with my niece's husband."

She nodded. "And it wouldn't be if it was," she said curtly.

"Maybe not," I said. "But I'd have more interest in making it my business."

She nodded as if entirely appreciating that, which rather surprised me. "Well, I'll tell you what I'm doing here." There was a sardonic glint in her eye. "I'm taking off ten pounds I put on while I've been in mourning—not dancing and not smoking, and eating too much, and stuffing candy and alcohol all day long to keep from dying of boredom and respectability. Now I've done my bit, and his family can't say I was just waiting for him to pop off before I started running out to night clubs again.—And Reno's the swellest place I know to do it."

She laughed. I've never, I think, heard so disillusioned and mirthless a sound as she made. She took out her compact and looked at herself in the mirror.

"Today I've had one hour steaming, one hour massage, two hours' horseback riding, three glasses of orange juice and two bunches of celery. Tomorrow I'll start eating again and take more massage. If you're my type you can't take it off starving without it making your face and neck look like stringy mutton."

I looked at her, not seeing where ten pounds could come off. But I've dieted enough myself to know that other people seldom do.

"I still don't see why you came to Reno to do it," I said —since she'd brought it up.

"No? Well, maybe because I haven't got any place else to go where I can have as good a time and no questions asked. Nobody cares here as long as you've got money to spend. I can have fun till I get remodelled, and then I'll go somewhere else."

She shrugged her shoulders. "Who knows?"

I picked up my check.

"It seems very barren and disillusioned to me," I said. "But I suppose you know what you want."

She nodded coolly. "And I know how to get it."

"Then that makes it just dandy," I said. "Good night."

She didn't answer. For some curious reason I had a sudden stab of pity for her that was pretty stupid, I suppose. She most certainly didn't want it, or need it. I glanced back from the door. She was sitting up at the long curving bar with a glass of orange juice in front of her, surrounded by a crowd of people that included Whitey and a couple of men I knew were lawyers, going through the paces with their new—and important—clients. She would do all right, I thought, going out into the cool fresh air into the silent streets, still bright and gaily lighted for all their emptiness.

14

I nodded to the detective who looked out of the linen room as I went by, and opened my door. I wasn't tired as much as I was deflated. I didn't want to go to bed. It occurred to me that that was probably why the River House was still crowded and hectic. People didn't want to go to bed and be alone with the sense of defeat and unrest, and the excitement of dashing about and drinking and gambling, even if it was just pulling the lever of a slot machine, kept them from it.

I opened Judy's door very quietly, and glanced in. She had put the Do Not Disturb sign on her door—I'd noticed it as I came in. The room was dark. I listened. I couldn't hear her breathing. I waited a minute, listening, a little chill gathering on my heart, and then threw open the door and turned on her light.

Her bed was pulled down from behind its door, but Judy wasn't in it. The long windows were open. For one terrible moment I stood there, the horrible thought of that river three stories below the balcony burning in my mind. Then, as I stood absolutely petrified, my eyes fell on a sheet of paper on the table in the middle of the rose-and-gray room. My knees felt like water as I crossed over to it, and steadied myself as I looked down and read.

"Dear Grace,—Don't be alarmed. I've had to go out a minute. Leave the window open. I'll be back.—J."

I sank down in a chair, shaking like a leaf. The phone jangling suddenly nearly scared me out of my wits. My hand shook as I lifted the receiver, and my heart stood still at the sound of a familiar voice.

"Mrs. Latham," it said, "—this is John Primrose. I've been trying to get you. Mrs. Bonner is up at Lake Tahoe. And I'm sorry to have to tell you, but I think you ought to know it— Hogan has put her under formal arrest.—Martin will call for you shortly."

I had a curious sense of running the gauntlet of a pack of jackals as I went downstairs, some minutes later, through the lobby and out into the street. Whitey and Kaye Gorman and Joe were there, standing at the bar. I saw them glance at me and at each other. Why Judy had let herself get mixed up with such people was beyond me, I thought suddenly. Why she couldn't have gone to a quiet civilized ranch out in the hills, the way her friend Polly Wagner had, and waited discreetly and patiently for her six weeks, I couldn't think. But of course I did know, really. She was upset and alone, and Dexter Cromwell had been her guide. Tomorrow she would go, bag and baggage, I thought . . . if by tomorrow she wasn't in the city jail.

Mr. Martin held the door of his car open for me, and closed it. "It was most imprudent of her, leaving the hotel at all," he said.

"I know. But it's what you have to expect. I haven't an idea why she did it."

"I imagine it had something to do with this business," he said. "Cromwell had a cottage up there. The thing that worries me is that it may interfere with her decree."

"That's not what's worrying me," I said.

We stopped in front of the Second Street entrance to the city hall. The Y. W. C. A. is in the basement, the police headquarters directly above. We went in. It had the musty smell of cleaning oil and wooden floors. I shuddered as we passed the desk, where a couple of night men were on duty, and went into the middle room. Three boys hardly out of their teens and a couple of women with hard faces and cheap flashy clothes were waiting, sullen and unpleasant. I wondered what Judy's mother, collapsed at the Ritz in London, would think of her daughter rubbing shoulders with erring humanity. But I needn't have. Bill Hogan, I found out, had taken her into the Chief's office from the corridor, so she had missed the desk and the furtive eyed boys and the women.

She was sitting beside the desk, her face as blank as a mask. Only a little flicker in her eyes indicated any feeling at seeing me.

Colonel Primrose, sitting on the desk, nodded to me.

"Mrs. Bonner," he said. "You know you are perfectly within your rights not to make any statement. But I have a feeling that it would help your situation for you to speak—not prejudice it."

"But there isn't anything for me to say," Judy said quietly. "I've already told Mr. Hogan I didn't see Dex Cromwell after I left the River House with Joe Lucas."

"You mean you didn't have a violent quarrel with him some time in the early morning before he was killed?"

Judy hesitated. She didn't look at me, and I tried desperately to look as if that meant nothing to me. The quixotic business of continuing to protect the man she was divorcing was getting pretty hard for me to bear.

"No. I didn't," she said.

"Then how do you account for this?"

Bill Hogan leaned forward with a piece of paper in his hand. It had been wadded up and smoothed out. He handed it to Judy. I leaned forward. My heart took a nose dive to the pit of my stomach. It was the note I'd sent her by the bell boy. I could remember without seeing it exactly what it said: "Judy dear—if you two will stop this insane quarrelling now, and resume at a more seasonable hour, you will please your devoted aunt who would very much like to get some sleep."

Judy handed it back to Mr. Hogan, her cheeks colorless.

"I can't explain it," she said.

"It was in your waste basket, Mrs. Bonner. One of the bell boys brought it from Mrs. Latham to your room around three o'clock in the morning."

Mr. Hogan did not look at me. Neither did Colonel Primrose.

"I have nothing to say," Judy said quietly.

Colonel Primrose looked at me.

"I must have made a mistake," I said.

Bill Hogan grunted. "Well, there's this, then."

He took a parcel out of a drawer in the desk and untied it. It was Judy's brown-spotted riding shirt. He unrolled it, and let the wrought iron candle pick with its stiletto point still crusted with clotted blood lie there on the desk in front of her.

Colonel Primrose looked at her gravely. "As you know, that was found in your clothes hamper.—Did you put it there, Mrs. Bonner?"

There's more than one admits nowadays in breeding. Judy didn't flinch.

"I didn't put it there, Colonel Primrose."

"Then—how did it get there?"

There was a gentleness in his voice that she recognized instantly. Her pale face brightened for an instant. She raised her moss-gray eyes to him.

"I don't know. Honestly—I really don't."

Hogan frowned. "If you'd be frank with us, Mrs. Bonner—"

"I am being frank, Mr. Hogan."

"Honest, then."

"And I'm being honest, too," Judy said quietly. "I didn't put it there—I haven't any idea of how it got there."

Colonel Primrose was looking steadily down at her from his perch on the side of the desk.

"If you'd tell us what you did do last night, Mrs. Bonner, it might help."

She looked at him with bewildered eyes.

"I didn't do anything, really! I mean . . . well, I went to dinner with my aunt and Mr. Cromwell. Mrs. Gorman and Joe Lucas joined us. Dexter and Mrs. Gorman left. I was sort of fed up with the whole place."

She rolled her crumpled handkerchief in a tight little wad in the palm of her hand.

"I suppose it sounds strange, but everything seemed . . . well, sort of different, after . . . she came." She nodded toward me without looking up. "I mean, it suddenly struck me as all being frightfully . . . well, tawdry, and stupid—and what was I doing it for. I never thought of it like that, but seeing my aunt . . . I mean, she's so appallingly normal, and . . . and well-bred, and . . . well, the rest of them weren't. Even Dexter Cromwell. He looked, all of a sudden . . . well, I mean he looked too . . . something. Sort of phoney, if you know what I mean. I just didn't want any more of it. I mean, my aunt hadn't said anything, but I could see that was what she thought—about Dex."

Colonel Primrose nodded. "And what did you do, Mrs. Bonner?"

"I went out for a drive, out to Truckee, with Joe Lucas. We came back a little after two. I talked to some people in the bar, for about half an hour. Then I went upstairs and stayed there for a while . . . till about half-past two. Then I . . . I went downstairs again. I couldn't bear being in that room alone, and I didn't like to bother my aunt. I was going for a drive, but they'd picked my car up. I keep it at a garage in Chestnut Street. I didn't want to bother them to bring it back."

I saw Bill Hogan glance at Colonel Primrose, a rather odd expression on his face.

"So I just walked along the river . . . just walked along, that's all, until about four. I came in and went to sleep. I was dreadfully tired."

The three men there looked at her. I could see perfectly plainly that none of them believed her. Even without the salvaged note of mine, and Mrs. de Courcey's report of the quarrel, I doubt if they would have done. It was too transparent, too childish.

Colonel Primrose took out a pack of cigarettes and held it down to her. She shook her head. He lighted one himself.

"How about yesterday afternoon, Mrs. Bonner?"

She looked up, waiting for him to explain.

"You knew your aunt was coming on the afternoon plane, didn't you?"

Judy nodded. Her face had closed again, as if someone had suddenly put up a pair of invisible shutters and barred them with invisible bars.

"Why didn't you go to meet her?"

"Because I had something else I had to do. I sent Dex Cromwell, only I didn't explain she wouldn't look like an aunt. So he missed her."

"Or perhaps meeting Mrs. Gorman was the cause of it?"

There was no sign of light, or anger, in her face. It was blank and locked.

"You had something else to do that was important enough to keep you from meeting Mrs. Latham?"

"Yes."

"What was it, Mrs. Bonner?"

"Nothing, really."

Mr. Martin's Bryanic face was very worried.

"It is a fact, isn't it, that you went to Virginia City, alone?"

"Yes."

"And bought that candle pick?"

She nodded without looking at it.

"The clerk at the shop, Mrs. Bonner, says you jabbed it in your stomach and said, 'This would make a grand dagger, wouldn't it?' "

The last vestige of color drained from Judy's face. Her lips moved, but no sound came from them.

"The clerk said, 'Yes, many a miner in the old days got one of these between the ribs.'—Do you remember his saying that to you, Mrs. Bonner?"

Martin jumped to his feet. "Don't answer that, Mrs. Bonner! Just a—"

Judy nodded slowly. "It's true. I did say that—so did he. But I didn't mean . . ."

"Who is Charles Baker, Mrs. Bonner?" Colonel Primrose asked abruptly.

If they were trying to catch her, it was a tactical error. She was still too stunned to be stunned any further. She just shook her head. "I don't know."

"He tried to call you all day yesterday, Mrs. Bonner," Bill Hogan said.

"I know. I got the slips they put in my mail box. But I didn't talk to him. I don't know anybody of that name."

Hogan took a paper out of his folder on the desk. "These are fingerprints from his room in the hotel, Mrs. Bonner.— And they match."

Judy looked up. I could see her clinching her fists to keep from crying out. Her voice was almost completely casual.

"Match—what?" she asked.

"Fingerprints on Dexter Cromwell's car door," Colonel Primrose said quietly.

There was no sign of shock or surprise in her face, no sign that she hadn't already known how it would be.

Colonel Primrose ran his hands through his thick gray hair —which I knew was a sign that he was more than a little puzzled.

Hogan took out another card. "We've broadcast this description of him. Well over six feet, broad shouldered, athletic. Between twenty-eight and thirty-two. Wavy chestnut hair, hazel eyes, tanned complexion, slight scar on forehead, wearing gray chalk stripe flannel suit and brown shoes.—He had a seat reserved on the Eastern plane, but he wasn't on it. Not when it reached Omaha, anyway."

Judy's eyes widened.

Colonel Primrose leaned forward and took her hands in his, looking her steadily in the eyes.

"Mrs. Bonner," he said, very earnestly, "did you, with these two hands, murder Dexter Cromwell?"

"No—she didn't!"

A hard quiet voice from the door brought every one of us to startled attention. I turned my head, but I'd seen in Judy's face already a valiant little standard flying, a mixture of all the emotions a woman knows. Before my eyes reached him I knew that the man standing there was well over six feet, with broad shoulders, hazel eyes, suntanned skin, with the scar on his forehead. And I well remembered the Harvard-Princeton game that he'd got that scar in.

I looked back at Judy. She was sitting back in her chair, her eyes closed; and I saw the tears crowding under her long gold-tipped lashes. She hadn't looked around.

"I heard on the radio you wanted me," the man said. He came on into the room. "Here I am. My name's Clem Bonner."

15

Clem Bonner came calmly in and sat down at the end of the desk opposite Judy. Bill Hogan's bright blue eyes were fixed intently on him. Colonel Primrose glanced at Judy Bonner, sitting there, staring at the floor, a smile flickering for a brief instant in his sparkling black parrot's eyes.

"Perhaps, Mr. Bonner," he said politely, "you'll be good enough to explain why you registered at the Washoe under a false name?"

Clem tossed his battered gray hat down on the desk. His jaw was set, his eyes sombre and unhappy, his mouth hard. My heart sank. I'd never seen him like this before. I'd known him chiefly as a friendly, grinning, charming young man usually coaching my two youngsters, who simply worship him, in broken field running—I imagine—across my back garden . . . something, certainly, that involved kicking up all the mulch carefully laid down for the winter.

He'd barely nodded to me, and he hadn't even glanced at Judy. He looked now at Hogan and Colonel Primrose, with steady unflinching eyes.

"So my wife wouldn't be made the subject of still more gossip," he said curtly.

The eyes of the two policemen rested on him, unwavering, probing.

"Yeh?" Hogan said. "You could have done that easier by keeping away from Reno. What'd you come out for?"

"I didn't like the company my wife was keeping. As long

as she is my wife, I'm doing what I can to take care of her."

"You mean Cromwell?"

"Right."

"You know he's dead—murdered?"

Clem nodded. "And it's O. K. as far as I'm concerned."

There was an instant of rather intense silence in the police headquarters of The Biggest Little City in the World. Clem pulled a battered pack of cigarettes out of his jacket pocket and lighted one, entirely indifferent to the sudden consternation in Judy's eyes.

Colonel Primrose glanced at me. When he spoke I knew he was being deliberately provocative.

"And you left the hotel, Mr. Bonner . . . knowing your wife would be bound to be involved?"

A kind of sardonic amusement flickered in Clem's eyes. "You can put it that way."

Judy's voice broke in, thrilling with sudden protest.

"But that's not true! He didn't know Dex was dead!"

Their eyes met, and held an instant. Clem said curtly, "You keep still."

The color flamed in Judy's cheeks, and died. I saw her catch her under lip in her teeth to keep it from trembling visibly.

"How do you explain your fingerprints on the car Cromwell was murdered in, Mr. Bonner?"

I saw Clem's eyes sharpen, his jaw tighten a little harder, as if this was something he was not prepared for. "I guess that's for you to figure out," he said coolly.

Colonel Primrose picked up the wrought iron candle pick on the desk. "Have you seen this, Mr. Bonner?"

A sharp wedge of silence thrust itself suddenly into the room. Judy's body tensed as if she were steeling herself for a blow.

"I haven't anything to say," Clem said abruptly. Colonel Primrose turned the bloodstained candle holder over in his hands as if he was examining it for the first time. Clem's eyes were fixed on it, and beyond it on Judy's crumpled and stained riding shirt.

"This is what he was killed with," Colonel Primrose said casually. I suppose nobody but Sergeant Buck and myself would have known that he was as tense and aware as a pointer motionless in the field. "It was found in Mrs. Bonner's clothes hamper in her bathroom, wrapped in this shirt of hers."

He picked the shirt up, deliberately, and wrapped the candle holder again.

The blood surged darkly into Clem's face. He started to

speak, and checked himself. Judy turned in her chair so that she didn't have to look at him. I had the feeling, as her body relaxed that the small white flame of . . . something, I didn't know what . . . had died again in her heart just then.

Colonel Primrose put the shirt-wrapped weapon back on the desk.

"Doesn't get us very far, does it?" he said placidly, and got up. "Well, I think Mrs. Bonner ought to get some rest."

He looked at Bill Hogan. Hogan pushed back his chair.

"We . . . don't like to keep a lady in the cells downstairs, Mrs. Bonner," he said gruffly. "It's up to you. If you'll go back to your hotel and stay there, all right. But you'll understand you're . . . incommunicado."

He looked at Clem, and at Mr. Martin. "She's in your custody, Martin. You can take her back."

Judy's face under its sun tan was the color of old ivory. "Thank you, Mr. Hogan!" she said, her low voice like the surface of rubbed velvet.

Clem Bonner got up, his eyes fixed on her for the first time, dumb and aching. I thought for a moment that he couldn't help crossing the room to her and crushing her in his arms, once and forever. But maybe I was mistaken. "I won't try to see her, if that's what you mean." He spoke so brusquely that her body stiffened involuntarily.

She hesitated as she passed me. "Are you coming, Grace?"

"I'd like Mrs. Latham to stay a minute," Colonel Primrose said. "You too, Mr. Bonner."

Judy went quickly out the door. I think I felt a more poignant ache for her just then, going out, chin up, back straight, her gray eyes almost blinded with unshed tears, than I've felt since the years I watched my two tiny boys meet their small reverses with the appallingly sturdy fortitude of childhood. A broken train of cars teaches people to take a broken train of dreams, I suppose.

Their steps, hers quick and light, Mr. Martin's slow and ponderous, died away in the night. Hogan nodded to Colonel Primrose and went out. Colonel Primrose shifted his position on the edge of the desk.

"I want to say something to both of you," he said calmly. "You might come a little closer, Mrs. Latham.—The amount of evidence that's piling up against Mrs. Bonner is pretty staggering. But—and it's against the rules of police procedure for me to tell you this—it's so damned staggering that both Hogan and the Chief of Police, as well as myself, have about come to the conclusion that it's too staggering."

He looked at us for a moment, his face very grave.

"On the other hand, the District Attorney, who's somewhat of an ass, and hasn't been in office very long, doesn't see that. And it's highly probable, the way things stand at present, that he could make a local jury not see it. Furthermore, he has political ambitions, and a case like this could make a good spring board."

Clem Bonner's face was expressionless.

"However, I . . . don't believe she killed him. In fact, since nine-thirty this evening I've been pretty certain she didn't."

He looked at me with a polite but sardonic smile, and I stared at him open-mouthed, trying desperately to think what could have happened at nine-thirty. It would have been just about the time I was trying to call Clem in New York from the Washoe bar.

He went on slowly.

"I don't think she killed Cromwell. There has to be a motive for doing things like that, and a powerful one. Wilstack —the District Attorney—thinks jealousy is enough, in this case. Perhaps. If it is, it won't be Mrs. Bonner we're looking for. She didn't care enough about the fellow to kill him."

He looked down at Clem Bonner for an instant.

"That brings up two possibilities, one of which is . . . unpleasant. Someone else killed Dexter Cromwell, with a motive that so far we are utterly in the dark about; and he deliberately put the murder off on Mrs. Bonner, perhaps because, in some way, it was just the simplest thing to do . . . or, more probably, because he had a very devilish determination that Judith Bonner was to suffer for it."

He stood up, his voice harder and more clipped than I'd ever heard it. "There are human emotions that turn into something pretty terrible, when they go sour. Murder is healthy, compared to that. The torture that whoever did this is putting Mrs. Bonner through is . . . not healthy."

Clem Bonner got up abruptly, and paced back and forth between the desk and the door.

Colonel Primrose watched him silently for a moment. "The point being," he went on coolly, "that you two have got to help me here. There are questions that must be answered, and quickly.—Assuming that Mrs. Bonner did not herself take that candle pick out of her room and put it back, stained with Cromwell's blood, in her clothes hamper, there is no problem about *how* that was done. Anybody could have got in her room quite easily by means of the corridor window and the fire escape. But who? And was Mrs. Bonner out at the race track with Cromwell when he was killed? And above all . . . *why* was he killed?"

I looked at him stupidly, not understanding . . . for the

only thing we really knew, Colonel Primrose and I, was that whatever else Judy Bonner had done or had not done, she had been there in the car when he had died. Those golden hairs clutched in his hand were silent and damning testimony to that.

He went calmly on. "And what about Mr. Bonner's finger-prints on the door of that car? Was he at the race track too?"

Clem Bonner, still pacing back and forth, halted abruptly.

"No," he said. "He wasn't. And Judy wasn't either."

Colonel Primrose nodded politely.

"Sure of that, Bonner?"

"Quite."

"Then you were with her after you saw Cromwell?"

My heart sank as Clem flushed darkly again.

Colonel Primrose shifted his weight on the desk. "Why *did* you come out here, by the way?"

"I've told you."

"You've told me part."

Clem turned angrily, or so I thought at first. I saw then that it wasn't anger as much as it was pain and resentment, struggling with new bitterness, and new doubt. He looked at Colonel Primrose for a long instant, coolly, steadily apprais-ing, before he answered.

"All right. Here's the rest of it. When my wife decided to come out here, I told her I'd give her a power of attorney so she could get her divorce, uncontested and decently, and marry Cromwell—if she wanted to, and that's what she did want—just as long as he didn't come out here with her. I told her that, and I told him too. I found out, three days ago, that he did come out with her . . . and I came out to break his God damned neck. That's why I came out."

I started violently at a deep voice that spoke suddenly from the door behind me: "Is this a confession, Bonner?"

I turned in my chair and stared aghast at the little man standing there behind me. He wore a bright brown suit, and he had a bald narrow domelike head and glittering black eyes as sharp and beady as shoe buttons, and a large rigid mouth in a thin saffron-colored face.

"Is this a confession?" he repeated harshly.

"This is Mr. Wilstack," Colonel Primrose said suavely. "The District Attorney.—Mrs. Latham, and Mr. Bonner."

The District Attorney's little beady eyes were boring into Clem's face. And Clem, startled for the moment, stared an-grily at him. "You can take it for one, if you like," he said curtly.

"Since your fingerprints are all over the door of the death car . . ." Wilstack began. He hesitated, a shadow of calculated indecision on his shrewd little face as he darted a glance at Colonel Primrose. "Come in here," he said abruptly. "I want to talk to you."

He held the door open. Clem gave me a quick sardonic grin and strode through.

I picked up my bag. Colonel Primrose was standing by the door leading to the corridor.

"I would never have believed," I said bitterly, "that you could have let anybody down like that."

I was terribly angry, at his doing that to Clem, and hurt too, I suppose.

He stared at me for a moment, puzzled, and then incredulous. Then he blocked the door, his hand on the knob, an expression of hurt bitterness gathering on his own face.

"You're at liberty to believe anything you choose, my dear," he said. "I'm only trying to save your niece. And if I do, it will be in spite of a large and varied multitude of perfectly demented things that you've done, Mrs. Latham . . . and if I fail, it will be because I can't untie the noose you've already tied around her neck."

I stared at him, blank-faced and utterly speechless.

"And inasmuch as I'm only doing this for you—"

He stopped abruptly. "Good night."

I hurried out and through the still brilliantly lighted empty streets . . . hurt, and bewildered, and unhappy, and more afraid, in spite of what he'd said before, than I'd ever been in my life.

Whitey and Kaye Gorman were at the hotel desk playing blackjack with the night clerk. They looked up as I came in, and Kaye came over to where I was standing by the elevator.

"Is it true Clem's back?" she asked.

I nodded.

"Where is he?"

"In jail, I imagine," I said. "He seemed to be heading that way."

"Are you being funny, Mrs. Latham?"

Her voice was hard, and irritated.

"I wish I could be," I said shortly. "Good night."

16

I don't know how late I should have slept the next morning if I hadn't been waked by something touching me. I opened my eyes to see Judy sitting cross-legged on the foot of my bed.

Her wide-set gray eyes met mine gravely. "—What happened to Clem?"

I sat up.

"I don't know. He told Colonel Primrose he came out to break Dex's neck, and the District Attorney overheard him."

She twisted her handkerchief into a tight string and let it unroll.

"Judy," I said. "I don't want to pry into your affairs, but I would like to know why you allowed Dex Cromwell to come out here with you, when you'd agreed not to? It doesn't sound like you, some way."

The color rose slowly in her cheeks.

"He didn't come with me. I didn't know he was coming. He was here when I got here—he drove out before I left, and met me at the train."

Her long gold-tipped lashes brushing her cheeks covered her darkening downcast eyes.

"I told him he couldn't stay. He said he'd only come out to see I was all right. And I was miserably lonesome. I . . . I guess any sort of excuse was good enough. He wasn't staying in Reno. He was up at Lake Tahoe, on the California side."

She got up.

"He kept saying he'd leave the next day. . . . But it was just as much my fault as his, and I didn't care if Clem did know about it. I thought it wouldn't hurt him to know somebody thought I was just as attractive as . . . as Kaye. Only . . . nobody did."

I looked at her, standing in the windows, young and almost unbearably lovely, the sun making her hair a nimbus of molten gold.

"I know it sounds stupid and petty now, Grace! But I didn't think Clem really cared . . . that he actually meant he wouldn't let me come out if Dex came. We'd said so many dreadfully cruel things to each other . . . and then, suddenly, it was just all too late. I'd . . . I'd want to say I didn't care if he saw Kaye, just so he'd let me . . . see him too. And then I'd see him, and I'd say something dreadful I didn't mean at all, just because I loved him so much. . . . It sounds crazy, but—"

"But unfortunately true," I said. "It's what most people do. —What happened here, the other night?"

"Oh, just more of the same," she said unhappily. "He tried to tell me he didn't know Kaye was out here. But Dex had seen them together—coming out of his room. They're both on the next floor."

"And . . . after that, Judy?" I asked quietly. I hadn't asked her before—I hadn't even wanted to ask her, point-blank—if she couldn't tell me what had happened that night. I knew now that I hadn't dared . . . not from the moment I'd taken those two hairs from Dexter Cromwell's dead rigid fingers. And she didn't answer me now, for the phone in her apartment rang just as I'd spoken. She came back in a minute.

"It's a girl I knew at school," she said. "She's at a boarding house in Mill Street. I was supposed to go to court with her to-day. I . . . I said I'd see if you'd go with her instead.— Would you, Grace? She's had a rotten time of it, on account of the baby. She's rather upset."

She looked at me beseechingly.

"When do I go?" I asked.

"It's set for ten."

I've wondered since, many times, whether it would have made any difference in what happened afterwards if I'd told Judy—as I felt so much like doing—that my coming to Reno had been on her behalf alone, and that I really didn't have the strength to take on her friends too. If I'd done that—for one thing—I wouldn't have met Mr. Tucker, and I wouldn't have seen Vicki Ray headed down the corridor toward the District Attorney's office.

I got dressed and met the girl. It seems strange, now, but I don't even remember her name. She was sweet and rather wan and not far from tears.

"I haven't really known till this morning if my husband was going to let me have his power of attorney," she said. "If I didn't get it, I'd have to stay a month longer, and I've got a job waiting for me in Los Angeles—my things are at the bus station already."

A gray nondescript little man, quite elderly, with white mustaches yellow at the ends and comparatively no teeth, followed us through the marble portico of the court house and up a broad staircase to the left. A brash young man, the girl's lawyer, met us on the second floor.

"Now then," he said briskly. "You've got your witness? Oh yes—hello, Mr. Tucker."

The little man with the yellow mustaches nodded. The girl and her lawyer went into consultation by the double doors of the court room. I waited patiently, glancing up at the thin black-and-gold hand across the corridor pointing a scrawny finger above a label "District Attorney's Office." Then I looked back at Mr. Tucker, wondering what Daumier would have done with this scene, and stared.

He was nervously motioning someone back down the stairs. I looked past him and saw that oddly enough it was Vicki Ray down there. She'd stopped half way up, her big white hat tilted back on her black curly head, her blue eyes narrowed, the most curious smile on her red lips.

Mr. Tucker wiped the perspiration off his forehead and tugged at his soft Sunday collar as if it was strangling him. Vicki stood there a moment, came jauntily up the stairs, passed Mr. Tucker without a word, glanced at the pointing black-and-gold finger, and went on down the corridor. Half way down it she turned and smiled at Mr. Tucker, and saw me. She stopped short, and then, with her customary debonair salute from the brim of the big white stetson, she came back.

"Hello," she said. "How's Mrs. Bonner?"

"She's fine," I said. "How are you?"

I spoke with an ease that I was far from feeling, for I was greatly puzzled by all this. It's strange, I suppose, considering how extraordinary a bearing it was to have on everything, that I wasn't still more puzzled, and even upset.

"First-rate, thanks." She cracked her black boot with her crop. "What's this I hear about Mr. Bonner being here all the time?"

"That's all I know about it," I said.

"I mean, is it true?"

I nodded.

"Is he here now?"

"Yes."

She glanced down the corridor and bit her full lower lip meditatively. "—Where could I see him?"

"My guess would be the city jail," I said.

She pushed her hat back and smiled. Then she gave Mr. Tucker, still standing there by the railing, a side-long glance.

"This is my landlord," she said suddenly. She waved him over with an imperative gesture. "Mr. Tucker, where was I night before last from one-thirty on?"

If Vicki Ray had been a slightly intoxicated but good-humored tigress, and Mr. Tucker a rabbit pinned to the ground with one playful paw, he could not have been more unhappy.

"You were at the house, Miss Ray," he stammered wretchedly.

She raised an airy hand to me. "You see?"

"Why do you keep on telling me this?" I asked sharply. "I'm beginning not to believe it."

She smiled that odd smile of hers and looked meditatively at Mr. Tucker again.

Some people came out of the court room—a girl with a sheaf of gardenias on her shoulder, and a crowd of other girls laughing and cheering and clapping a young man on the shoulder.

"Come on down to the wedding, Vicki!" somebody shouted.

She gave them her breezy salute and turned back to me. "I'll be seeing you!" she said. I started to say something, and stopped cold . . . for as our eyes met I saw something behind her long black lashes that I had not thought could be there. It was fear—as plain, naked, ugly fear as I've ever seen in my life.

We stood there, staring silently at each other, for just that instant. The girl's lawyer said, "We're going in now," and I followed them to the judge's chamber. At the door I looked back. Vicki was going down the stairs, her boots clattering on the marble. I glanced at Mr. Tucker. His hands on his panama hat were shaking.

I don't remember much of that divorce trial. I listened to the girl I'd come with swear that she had lived in Reno since some date six weeks before, and that she expected and intended to reside in Nevada permanently. It seemed a trifle odd, in view of the fact that she had her bus ticket in her bag and her things at the station and a job waiting for her in Los Angeles, but everybody, including her husband's lawyer and the judge, was not only polite but solemn about it. Mr. Tucker swore to the fact that she had lived six weeks consecutively in Reno; he had seen her at least once in every twenty-four hours of that period. The grounds for divorce were simple too. Her husband stayed away nights. Once when he came home she had asked him where he had been, and he had told her it was none of her business. Her health had suffered under such extreme cruelty.

It was all over in eleven minutes by my wrist watch, and we went out and downstairs. Vicki was gone. I was still wondering about her, in a helplessly bewildered and even slightly frightened way—I couldn't get that look in her eyes out of my mind. I shook hands with the girl, who said, "Thank you

for coming with me, I was afraid he might be there—tell
Judy good-bye," and watched her get into a taxi and head for
Los Angeles.

The crowd I'd seen come out of the court room burst out
of the Riverside Bar with a great deal of laughing and cheering and throwing of rice and old shoes. How those two young
people had got married, and everybody half lit, in so short a
time, I couldn't say, but they had.

I crossed the sun-drenched street and went into the
Washoe. Sergeant Buck was in the lobby, and just in the act
of scooping an enormous number of half-dollars out of the
bottom of one of the slot machines. He gave me a bitter
glance out of that mahogany face. "The Colonel wants to see
you, ma'am," he said. "He's in 321."

I started for the elevator and stopped, hearing my name
spoken. It was Cowboy Joe, coming from the bar, a friendly
grin on his bronzed face.

"You seen Vicki this mo'nin', Miz' Latham?"

"Yes," I said. "I just saw her, at the court house."

His grin widened. "Don' tell me she's gettin' anoth'
divo'ce?"

"I couldn't say," I said.

A second voice broke in behind me. "Who's gettin' another
divorce?"

It was my friend Whitey, with his pale eyes and almost
albino hair. He still had on the same tan jodhpurs and salt-
sack polo shirt he'd worn at the airport when I came, and in
fact I never did see him in anything else, at any hour of the
day or night, through all my Reno visit.

"Unless she's gettin' married," Joe Lucas drawled. "Ain'
nothin' else Vicki'd be doin' at the co't house."

That scrawny black-and-gold finger pointing to the District Attorney's Office flashed into my mind just as Whitey
snapped his fingers with a sharp whistle. "Hey, maybe she
was payin' a call on old Button Eyes, which got her divorce
free on account she was cleaned out playin' blackjack the first
week she got here!"

I was abruptly aware that the figures moving in front of
me in one of the Washoe's mirrored pillars had stopped moving. For an instant it was almost as if I had in front of me a
stilled kaleidoscopic picture of my own mind . . . as it had
gone from person to person connected with Dexter Cromwell, trying, desperately, to find one—not my niece or her
husband—who was his murderer. For coincidence—perhaps
—had brought together here everybody . . . every person
who could possibly have had any reason to thrust that miner's
candle pick into Dexter Cromwell's throat . . . and was

holding them all, for an instant, motionless in the mirrored pillar.

Whitey and Joe Lucas and myself were closest to it. Beyond us, at the door of the bar, Eddie, the old-young waiter, stood, his eyes riveted, for some reason, on Whitey. The door of the elevator had opened at just that moment, and Mrs. de Courcey stood in it with her brace of dachshunds. Kaye Gorman was at the desk, her mail in her hands, her head turned, listening. Coming out of the phone booth beyond the desk, a fat special delivery airmail letter in her hand, her cheeks flushed, eyes shining, was Polly Wagner, in blue jeans and white shirt. Beyond Kaye, at the door, stood Mr. Tucker; and through the revolving door at just that moment, her own debonair self, came Vicki Ray.

And above all of it I could see the hard-bitten granite face of Sergeant Buck by the slot machines, his fishy gray eyes fixed sleepily on one of the men by my side.

I couldn't explain how, for that instant, all those people stayed motionless, as if they were electric robots, and then looked, each of them, as if still under some remote control, at the girl in the door.

She came on in, her head up, her broad white hat tilted back, smiling that oddly veiled and enchanting smile, strode airily through the lobby, raising her hand in her unique breezy gesture, and stepped into the elevator as Mrs. de Courcey stepped out. If the Mona Lisa hanging on her Louvre wall should wink at the crowd of trippers clustered in front of her, it would come nearer to Vicki's farewell salute to all of us in the lobby than anything I know.

17

Mrs. de Courcey's dachshunds broke the tension, straining at their leash and yapping like a pair of animated little sausages. Their mistress was in proper riding clothes, and looked as if she hadn't slept for weeks. But so, I thought, catching a glimpse of myself in the mirror, did I, and so did all of us.

"What about comin' out to th' ranch fo' a ride this evenin', Miz' Latham," Cowboy Joe drawled lazily. "Ah've got English saddles, if you don' like West'n."

"I'll see," I said.

He crossed the lobby to the desk, Whitey at his heels, and they went out with Kaye Gorman, Sergeant Buck eyeing them with a sort of fishy distaste . . . though Heaven knows he was at least infinitely gaudier than they were, in his bright orange shirt and jewelled boots. He put a half-dollar in the slot and pulled the lever. I heard the clatter of silver in the trough, and Polly Wagner's gay young voice:

"Sergeant . . . you're marvellous! I bet you've got a *system!*"

Sergeant Buck—and never would I have believed it if I hadn't seen it with my own eyes, and maybe the mirror I was seeing him in was distorted, the way they are in Palaces of Fun—flushed a vivid brick-red, and grinned like a very hard-bitten but sheepish schoolboy. Not all women, I was pleased to see, were his natural enemies . . . only me, and of course anyone else obviously laboring to ensnare the Colonel.

But that was not the oddest thing that happened just then. Sergeant Buck took one fishy glance around the lobby, burrowed suddenly into his gaudy Western integuments, pulled out something that looked to me very much like a letter, and slipped it into Polly Wagner's hand. And she, with only a quick glimmer of surprised relief, thrust it into the pocket of her levi's without a word, and sauntered over toward me in front of the elevator. Sergeant Buck, his frozen visage quite normal again, moved on in his iron way to the next slot machine.

Polly took hold of my arm and gave it a little squeeze, smiling up at me with her rather shy friendly eyes.

"Is Judy in her room?"

"I suppose so," I said. "If you can get in, tell her I'll be along after a bit, will you?"

We got out on the third floor. I went along to 321 and knocked. Colonel Primrose opened the door and said "Come in"—I thought rather shortly. He drew up a chair in front of the sofa.

"Hogan's got some information over the teletype I thought you'd be interested in," he said. "Cromwell's father is a banker in the sense that he's doorman at the Commonwealth Corn Exchange Bank in Milwaukee. His mother—you recall he told Judy he adored her and she died when he was sixteen, throwing him on his own because he couldn't get along with his despotic male parent—is alive and runs a rooming house. Cromwell went to high school and had one year on a football scholarship at a college near Milwaukee. His first wife was a widow with some money. He went through most of it and got a Reno divorce three years ago—by default. That means it's not recognized in most states. But that's neither here nor there. The point is that Cromwell was a smooth customer on the make, with a good many people hating him like poison, probably.—From the woman he married and rooked out of her investments—"

"Colonel Primrose!" I said. "You're not going to tell me that Cromwell's first wife has turned up, and she's a chambermaid in this hotel, and that—"

He chuckled.

"The nearest we've come to that is a girl who works in a beauty shop in Sierra Street who spent a lot of time, apparently, at a cottage he had at Tahoe, on the California side. He stayed there after he got his divorce."

I don't know why that reminded me of something.

"Have you seen Vicki?" I asked.

He shook his head. "Why?"

"She's got something on her mind."

He smiled dryly.

"We'd find it hard to get off, probably. That young woman has an amazing lot of pretty intimate friends—including the District Attorney. She also has a water-tight alibi for the night of Cromwell's murder . . . in spite of the fact that Buck saw her at four in the morning playing faro at a Chinese joint in Peavine Street."

I looked at him blankly.

"Don't let Vicki's breezy charm fool you, Mrs. Latham," he said, with a half smile.

He got up and went to the window, and looked out for a minute. Then he turned back. "They're holding the inquest this morning. It won't amount to much. I assumed you'd like to keep out of it, so I'm acting as witness."

He was looking at me gravely, and I knew, of course, that he was thinking about the red-gold hairs that I'd taken from Dex Cromwell's dead hand.

"I'm sorry if I was unduly abrupt last night," he said seriously.

"It doesn't matter," I said. "What happened to Clem?"

"He was released last night."

He was still looking at me.

"They're not letting him leave, but they're interested in the testimony of a waiter who lives out by the race track. He heard a woman running, around two. Even Wilstack can't think Clem's Number 10 shoes and one hundred-and-ninety pounds could sound like a woman running.—Incidentally, there's a strong impression, on Mr. Wilstack's part, that if Mrs. Bonner wasn't that woman, you were."

"*I* was . . . ?" I gasped.

"You, my dear. You didn't want your niece to marry Cromwell. You came out here—and the night you came, Cromwell was murdered. You did at least one definite thing that I could add, and haven't . . . so far. Oh, you'll give them rope enough to hang you with, before you're through."

He came and sat down on the sofa beside me.

"—And I'm much too fond of you to let them teach you a lesson you roundly deserve . . ."

I had the sudden quite ridiculous idea that he would have taken one of my hands if they hadn't been thrust inelegantly into the pockets of my tan linen jacket. He looked at me very earnestly, and said, "You know, Grace—" . . . and he never calls me that. But that's as far as he got.

The door burst open. Sergeant Buck's dead pan thawed just long enough for him to cast his chief a pained and reproachful glare. "Come in, Mr. Hogan—the Colonel ain't busy," he said.

I thought there was some annoyance in Colonel Primrose's black eyes.

Bill Hogan nodded briefly to me. "Look here, Colonel," he said. "There's something screwy going on around here."

Colonel Primrose's eyes sharpened.

"There's a man named Steve Ewing, been hanging around here for a couple of months. This morning when the maid was doing the next room she heard him groaning. I was down the hall and they called me, and I went in. Colonel, the fellow's had the living hell beat out of him! He's a wreck, and the place is a wreck. Two cameras in there smashed to pieces —swell cameras, too. And there's been a fire in the waste basket in the bathroom."

Colonel Primrose looked at him silently for a moment.

"Is he hurt—bad?"

"He'll live. He'll never be pretty again."

"Clem Bonner?"

Hogan shook his head.

"That's what makes it screwy. Bonner was on a plane over the Sierras when it happened. The woman in the room below heard a racket up there just after ten last night."

Colonel Primrose looked meditatively at the toe of his boot. His glance then rested casually on me, and then, just as casually, on the granite façade of his guard, philosopher and friend Sergeant Phineas T. Buck. The side of Boulder Dam before the water flowed through it was a mobile grinning mask compared to that face.

"I don't understand it," Colonel Primrose said. "Do you figure he was connected with Cromwell?"

Hogan nodded. "Cromwell's phone number was on his pad. The China boy at Tahoe says he's been up there a couple of times. It's got me beat, so far. Well, I'll be getting after it."

He went out. The silence in the room was definitely oppressive.

"I think I'll be going," I said, hastily.

I took a look back as I went out. Colonel Primrose's eyes were resting very steadily on the iron visage of his sergeant.

"You didn't tell me . . ." he began, and shrugged his shoulders.

I couldn't hear what else he said as I closed the door, but I could hear Sergeant Buck's grim voice through the door: "That louse ain't liable to talk, sir."

18

I went along the hall to my room and tossed my hat on the bed. The door leading to Judy's sitting room was open, and I could hear Polly Wagner's voice.

"So that's that, darling. And look, Judy . . . it's not any of my business, but the trouble with you, darling, is that you just don't know anything about Life."

I stood there, just frankly listening.

"I mean, if you'd had a husband who was never . . . never himself, and who . . . well, who had everybody in the house so terrified that no servant would stay, and my Scotty got so he'd crawl under the sofa when he heard his voice, and if we had guests I never knew whether there was going to be a horrible scene . . . And here, just because Clem took his first wife out to lunch . . . And you know I bet—that's me going Western . . . I hope I leave that out here with the levi's and these silly boots—I bet if you hadn't had Dex Cromwell always telling you how lovely and neglected and forlorn you were, sweetie pie, it wouldn't ever have entered your head. Anyway, you've got that, and I do hope it teaches you a lesson. And look, Judy—is your aunt going to marry Colonel Primrose?"

I started hastily to go, and then stopped.

"Don't be silly, darling," Judy said loftily. "She's much too young, and she has much too good a time. And, anyway, what could they do with Sergeant Buck? I mean it would be like having the Great Stone Face sitting in the chimney corner. You'd go absolutely nuts."

"Well, I think he couldn't be nicer," Polly said flatly.

"Colonel Primrose?"

"No, no—the Great Stone Face."

I did move then, as it occurred to me abruptly that I had something to do besides listen to a discussion of my matrimonial prospects and possible encumbrances . . . for it had been in the back of my mind ever since Colonel Primrose had made one certain remark, down the corridor there in his apartment, that the more definitely those bright red-gold hairs that I'd pulled out from under Dex Cromwell's hands on the wheel of that car were disposed of, the better, and that I might just as well do it, definitely, before Colonel Primrose asked me for them again.

I picked up a box of matches, went into the bathroom, took my riding shirt off the hook behind the door where it hung under my dressing gown, unbuttoned the pocket, took out my handkerchief. And then I stood there, the shirt in my left hand, the handkerchief still in my right, holding the pocket open, staring down into it. The red-gold hairs . . . so unmistakably from Judy Bonner's bright head . . . were not there.

I turned the pocket inside out, and turned the handkerchief over and over, my heart a solid lump of ice, my hands shaking uncontrollably. The hairs were gone.

I put the riding shirt on the hook again, went back into my room and sat down by the window, trying desperately to think what could have happened, my heart still stone-cold, my head still swirling. It was still swirling a minute later when the phone rang.

It was Clem Bonner. "Grace," he said, "—would you mind coming to my room? I've got to talk to you."

I pulled myself together, trying with a supreme effort to collect my scattered and terrified wits, and went on up to his room. He was in his shirt sleeves, pacing back and forth, and he looked like a man who had been through hell.

"I'm going crazy," he said.

I sat down on the side of the bed. I couldn't tell him that in all probability I had just delivered his wife, neatly bound with her own golden hairs, over to the police, and that I was about on the point of going crazy too.

"My God, I've got to talk to Judy! I've got to make her understand!"

"Understand what?" I demanded.

He began pacing again.

"Everything," he said, half-desperately. "I'm not blaming her, Grace. But I was damned if I was going to let that so-and-so have her. I thought if she got out here away from him, she'd come to.—I'm not blaming her for falling for him.

They all did. He didn't have anything to do but hang around, riding and dancing with her, while I was grubbing away down town. I was sore at first—I didn't think she was that sort. And she isn't, really. She's nothing but a kid . . ."

"And what about you and Kaye Gorman?" I inquired caustically. "Was that part of the down town grubbing?"

He glared at me.

"My God, yes!—I saw a lot of her, after Gorman died. There's no mystery about it, Grace! We had a lot of his private business, and we couldn't afford to lose it. When Kaye cashed in, half a dozen firms went after her. She came to town, and she had to be lunched and dined and so on. You know how it is. I had to do it when nobody else was on hand. She wasn't anything to me . . . and God knows I wasn't anything to her, after we'd lost everything. Well, I tried to explain to Judy. She seemed to understand, at first, and then she got up on her high horse, and then I got on mine . . . and first thing I knew I was hearing about Cromwell every place I went. And then I woke up one morning and found I'd lost her.—I guess I never knew how much I . . . loved her, before that."

He stopped and stared bitterly down at the carpet.

"I was damned if that lizard was going to come out here with her. I told him if he did I'd kill him."

"And . . . he did, and you did?" I inquired.

He turned on me, his face darkly flushed. Before he could say anything there was a rap at the door. He gave me one angry glare, strode over and opened it.

Vicki Ray was standing there, smiling, her white hat tilted back on her head.

"Hello!" she said. Then she saw me sitting on the side of the bed.

"Maybe Mrs. Latham will introduce us, Mr. Bonner," she said, and quite shyly, to my surprise. "Because I've got something to talk to you about."

I got up. Everything for the last twenty-four hours had made so little sense, as far as I was concerned, that this seemed perfectly real, and natural, and even obligatory.

"This is Miss Ray, Mr. Bonner," I said. "I'll see you both later."

The detective standing against the wall at the end of the corridor nodded to me as I went past. A cold shiver went down my spine, and an idea struck me at the same moment.

"Mr. Yerkes," I said—having remembered his name from the day before—"wouldn't you do me an enormous favor? It's compounding a felony, probably, but—"

I smiled as sweetly as I could manage.

He grinned dubiously. "Well, it all depends, ma'am," he said politely.

"My niece," I said, "is out here, as you know, for a divorce. I'm very sure that she and her husband are really still very much in love with each other. If they could only see each other a few minutes, I think it would save a lot of grief. Couldn't you go down for a drink, or something, and let him come and see her?"

Mr. Yerkes scratched his head. He was genuinely touched.

"Listen, Mrs. Latham. It ain't regular—but you tell her she can go up and see him. I ain't supposed to let anybody but her lawyer go in her room.—That young lady that was down there went in *your* room."

"Thank you!" I said. "She can't go for a little while—he's busy, right now."

"Whenever she's ready. I'll be reading."

I went on down the hall and into Judy's room. It didn't, as I'd known all the time, make the slightest difference that Vicki Ray was at present in Clem's room, for it took me fifteen minutes to persuade Judy to go up there. I told her, patiently, over and over again, everything Clem had said, and pointed out just as many times that he couldn't come to her, because he'd promised the police he wouldn't and anyway it was opposed to Mr. Yerkes' orders. Then at last I watched her go down the hall, head up, past where Mr. Yerkes was absorbed in the morning paper out of somebody's waste basket.

And I'd closed the door and taken, I think, the first full breath of relief I'd drawn all day, and gone to the window and stood there in the sunshine, looking down at the Truckee, for perhaps two minutes, when the door behind me opened and shut again so sharply that I whirled around.

Judy was standing against it, her face white.

"Judy!" I said. "What is it?"

She raised one hand and pushed her bright hair slowly back from her forehead, took a long breath and came unsteadily into the room. "Nothing—really."

She was trying to make her voice perfectly casual, and failing, so miserably!

I knew Clem Bonner couldn't have said much to her—there hadn't been time. I put my arm around her. She let her head touch my shoulder.

"She was there—just going in," she whispered. "Kaye."

She shook her head and tried to laugh. "In a beautiful ice-blue satin negligée. I . . . I guess I'm not feminine enough. —But don't be upset! It's . . . quite all right!"

19

Sometimes now, quite safe at home in Georgetown, I wake up at night and hear the death rattle of the wind in the last sear leaves of the tulip poplar outside my window . . . and the whole of my next two days in Reno flashes dreadfully through my mind, as the memory of the rack must forever have tortured the dreams of a man escaped from the Inquisition. And I can still see Judy Bonner, so plainly, standing there in her gray linen frock, white and shaken, the yellow sun burning on her red-gold hair, staring dry-eyed out of the window.

I had less than no idea of what to say to her, and I was more than grateful when the telephone rang suddenly in the complete silence of the hot room. It was Mr. Martin. For some reason that I did not comprehend, and that I don't think Mr. Martin did either, but that apparently had some connection with the inexplicable mauling of a man in the hotel named Ewing, Mrs. Bonner was released from technical arrest. She was at liberty—temporarily—to come and go as she pleased, provided she did not attempt to leave Reno.

I hung up and repeated that to Judy. She stood at the window for a long time, as if she hadn't heard, or hearing, didn't care. At last she crossed the room to the phone and called the garage for her car. "I think I'll go for a long drive, out in the desert," she said.

I followed her to the door and watched her go down the corridor. As I turned back I heard Mrs. de Courcey's usually brisk voice rise stridently: "That's nothing but blackmail!" Someone answered—whether man or woman I couldn't make out. And as I couldn't very well just stand there with my ear practically at her keyhole, I closed my door, wondering a little, and went back to Judy's sitting room. I sat down at her desk, reached in the drawer for some paper, and set out on the letter to her parents that had got to be written sooner or later.

I wrote one page, and came to a dead stop. The page underneath had been written on. I should have had to be both blind and not a woman not to have read what was on it. It said:

"Dear Dex—I meant what I said, last night. You may be

right that Vicki doesn't matter. Mrs. de Courcey's different. She's . . ."

And it stopped. I sat there looking at it for a long time. Then I took it and the couple of sheets underneath over to the fireplace, held a match to them, and crushed the ash out on the hearth. I went back to my letter, and I was still writing —it wasn't an easy letter to do—an hour later when the phone rang again. It was Judy—she and Polly Wagner were at the River House, and wanted me to come and have dinner with them.

It seemed to me that everybody in Reno was crowded into that dark little hole that night. Kaye Gorman and Joe Lucas were propped up on high stools at the bar when I went in, Kaye in a stunning black lace evening dress. Mrs. de Courcey and Whitey were with a little crowd around the roulette wheel. I don't know whether, in the crowd and the noise, Judy saw Clem Bonner come in. Polly did, and so did I, and Kaye Gorman and the rest of them. Judy probably did, because she noticed Colonel Primrose and Sergeant Buck . . . coming in, to my surprise, with Vicki Ray in a white fur coat.

Colonel Primrose, with a smile at Vicki, joined Mrs. de Courcey at the roulette wheel. I saw Vicki stop by the piano, where a little crowd gathered around a girl in blue jeans and Western boots who was twirling a rope that I supposed belonged to one of the cowboys getting ready for the Rodeo. They were laughing and passing the rope around until almost everybody had gathered there, except Mrs. de Courcey and Colonel Primrose and ourselves, and then the orchestra came in and they all broke up into couples and began dancing.

I'm not sure how long we sat there over our dinner. Judy got up suddenly and wandered away across the floor. I looked around. Clem was talking to one of the bartenders, but his sombre eyes were following Judy in the mirror, as if they would never see anything else when she was near. She went back toward the cocktail lounge in the gallery that overlooks the Truckee, and disappeared through the swinging doors. I looked for Colonel Primrose. He had moved along and was playing twenty-one with Benny the senior River House dealer. Sergeant Buck had retired to the bar.

I don't know why I should have had a strange and frightened feeling in my heart as I sat there . . . as if all this gaiety was unreal, and in some way wrong. I don't know now whether I really had some sort of prescience of what was going to happen, or whether it was just an excess of the feeling I found I nearly always had, after the first, in spite of everything, in Reno night clubs. The dealers and bartenders, the managers and maîtres d'hôtel, the head waiters, shills and come-on men had sharp and calculating eyes pinned on their guests, and the bland or cheery smile that instantly appeared if they saw you looking at them had so much of what the District Attorney would call the cat and mouse angle that it was a little morbid.

After a while Judy came back. She didn't dance, but just sat there, pretty silently, for ten or fifteen minutes, I suppose. And all of a sudden—and again I don't know why, except that it often happens to me—all of this became impossibly oppressive. It occurred to me in the most irresistible way that if I didn't get away from the noise, and the clack of chips, and the clink of glasses on the bar, I'd go quietly mad.

I got up and went across the dance floor. The doors of the cocktail lounge were closed. I pushed them open and stepped inside. The dimly lighted nooks around the room were quite empty. Behind me the orchestra leader was singing a semi-naughty song dedicated on the spur of the moment to the girl who'd been doing the rope trick, who'd apparently just got her decree that afternoon. The doors closed behind me, blotting all that out for a moment, and then I heard them open again, and glanced back.

Colonel Primrose had followed me out. He took hold of my arm.

"Come and sit down," he said. "I want to talk to you—seriously."

He nodded toward the leather upholstered nook in the far corner. I took a step, and tripped on something. He steadied me till I got my balance. We both looked down.

Stretching taut across the floor, wound a couple of times around the heavy chromium pedestal of one of the cocktail tables, was a rope. I looked down at it, in the half-dark of the room, not understanding, bewildered, and with some kind of a vague, reasonless chill suddenly on my heart. Then my heart gave a quick plunge as Colonel Primrose's hand tightened abruptly on my elbow, and he caught his breath sharply.

"Stay here . . ." he said. He pushed me back a little with one hand, and took a step toward the end of the room, where that taut rope led. And I followed him, and looked around his shoulder when he stopped suddenly. It was very dark at that end of the room, by the River, but by the bright lights along the bridge and the white, pink and blue glow of the Riverside Hotel sign, I could make out a mass of black lace, huddled limp and dreadfully motionless against the yellow leather of the curving seat . . . and on the seat too, just visible under the edge of the table there, and held down at a

horrible angle by a turn of the rope around that second pedestal, a white throat . . . around it, biting into the swollen
flesh, the noose, taut and strangling.

For an incredible instant that seemed eternity we both
stared down in horror. Then I heard my voice in an agonized
and terrified cry: *"Oh, God, it's Kaye Gorman!"*

Colonel Primrose moved sharply forward, bent down,
pulled desperately at that rope around the white throat.

"Get Buck!" he barked at me.

I couldn't have moved . . . but I didn't have to. Sergeant
Buck was already coming through the swinging doors. The
thought flashed through my mind, ludicrous even in that moment, that he'd seen his Colonel follow me into the deserted
and semi-dark room.

He came across from the door in three strides, pushed me
roughly aside, ripped a knife out of his cowboy belt, slashed
through the rope by the white throat, loosened the noose. He
lifted the limp black lace form round the table.

As the girl's body slumped down against the yellow leather
again—almost, I thought dreadfully, like a living figure—her
head rolled back against the seat.

I heard Colonel Primrose's sharp exclamation. And I stood
there, staring past him, shaking violently, unable to say a
word, or to think. It wasn't Kaye Gorman. I was looking
down on the blue-black hair and pitiful, once lovely face of
Vicki Ray.

20

I have the vaguest, sickest memory of the rest of that night
—of the people who came pouring in through the swinging
doors when they heard that cry of mine . . . and chief
among them Kaye Gorman herself, in the black lace dress
that had made me make that mistake.

She stared at me, her baby face white as death, as if in
some way she already saw the incredible significance that this
scene was to have before we were through.

"I . . . I thought it was you," I managed to say.

She shook her head—unnecessarily.

"They just haven't got around to me yet," she said. She
was trying to be indifferent and cynical, but her face was
dreadfully white and her hands shook as she lighted a cigarette.

Colonel Primrose's face was very grim. "All of you go back in there, and stay," he said curtly. He looked around. "Buck!"

There was a commotion outside, and Sergeant Buck came violently through the swinging doors. He had two men with him, each by the nape of the neck, like some monstrous Puss-in-Boots moving its kittens.

"Tryin' to sneak out through the kitchen, sir," he said composedly, out of the corner of his mouth.

I stared at them. One was my friend Whitey, the other Vicki Ray's landlord, Mr. Tucker. Both were shaking and terrified.

"I never done it!" Whitey screamed. "I swear to Jesus I never! I ain't seen her all night! I swear I ain't!"

"Get them out in the other room," Colonel Primrose said. "I am a special investigator—I'm in charge here till the police come. Get somebody at each door, Sergeant. See that nobody leaves and get the name of each person.—You can stay here."

He was looking—rather oddly—at Mr. Tucker when he said that. Mr. Tucker's face was ashy-gray around his yellowish mustaches.

The lounge emptied until only Colonel Primrose and I and Mr. Tucker were left. Then I noticed Clem Bonner, behind me by the windows overlooking the Truckee. He was standing as if he had taken root there, the ash hanging intact almost the length of his cigarette.

"What's on your mind, Bonner?" Colonel Primrose said abruptly.

Clem turned slowly, the ash splattering on the gold carpet. "Nothing," he said. He turned again and stood, staring out of the windows into the garish white-and-pink-and-blue night.

I moved over by him as Bill Hogan arrived . . . fear creeping about in my heart like a tiny yellow lizard in an empty cabin in the desert. The coroner was with him. They stood looking down at Vicki for an instant, raised her head, let it fall back, touched her hand.

"She hasn't been dead half an hour," Colonel Primrose said. He looked around. "There must be some other way out of here."

Hogan went to the swinging doors. In a moment Sergeant Buck appeared with one of the waiters, a Swiss named Ferdinand.

"Yes, sir. There's a door there, goes to the kitchen, and that door goes to the powder room."

He pointed to a panel in the wall to the left, and to another across the room behind a tub of palms.

"So anyone could go from this lounge directly to the bar

and dining room, or indirectly through the kitchen, or through the powder room?"

"Yes, sir. Or they could go out through the service entrance in the alley."

Mr. Tucker's hands shook violently.

"What are you doing here, Tucker?" Hogan asked.

"Somebody called up one of the ladies at my house . . . I came to see if I could find her . . ."

I don't know why I felt no twinge of sympathy for Mr. Tucker. His face was ashy-white as he babbled away incoherently, and he was certainly more abject than many of the things I find myself instinctively rising to defend. I suppose it was because there was something furtive about him.

"Vicki lived at your place, didn't she?"

Mr. Tucker nodded wretchedly.

Colonel Primrose turned to Buck. "Where was he?"

"In that passage out there, sir. He and this Whitey were fightin' to get ahead of each other at the alley door. I was lookin' after the other bird is how I happened to catch him."

"Take him off to the station," Hogan said curtly. Mr. Tucker's voice rose to a scream as a detective led him away through the panel to the right: "But I wasn't ever out of the passage!"

I watched Colonel Primrose looking down at the soft folds of black chantilly lace trailing over the yellow leather seat to the floor. "Find out whose rope that is," I heard Bill Hogan say.

"That's Ben Tavish's—a lot of them were doing tricks with it before the orchestra came in."

Hogan turned to another of his men. "Find out who were doing tricks with it. See how many cowpokes—professionals and gentlemen—were in there. It isn't everybody can throw a rope."

"The rope wasn't thrown," Colonel Primrose said quietly. "Not over the back of this booth. She was sitting here facing the river. You'll probably find she'd had a good deal to drink. Somebody came in with the rope . . ."

He stopped abruptly, staring down at the dead girl, and shrugged. I saw Clem Bonner, still by the windows at the end of the room, move slightly.

"A terrible chance to take . . . but this is a killer who's willing to take terrible chances."

He looked out through the open doors at the bar, where the little group from the Washoe were gathered trying to keep Whitey quiet. I looked for Judy. She and Polly Wagner and a couple of men dressed in Western clothes were sitting at a table in the dining room. It flashed into my mind that I was very glad I'd burned that unfinished letter. Whatever connection there might be between Judy and Dex Cromwell, there could be none apparent—with that letter burned—between her and the dead girl.

"We'll have a look," Hogan said grimly. He took his atomizer out of its black wooden box, sprayed the glass table top with a gray-green powder, and whistled. The side on which Vicki Ray had sat was covered with prints of many hands. The side near the doors was wiped clean.

"The rope was slipped over her head, jerked tight, looped around the pedestal," Colonel Primrose said. "Her head was drawn down on the seat. She was absolutely helpless. She hadn't a chance in the world, even if she'd been sober. The murderer then coolly anchored the rope end to the table over there on his way out. It wouldn't have taken a minute. In fact it was all over—practically—in thirty seconds. Any noise would be drowned by all that clatter outside. The killer then simply went back—through the passage to the alley and through the front door again, or through the kitchen, or through the powder room."

Hogan shook his head. "The powder room's out. A man wouldn't risk getting caught in there."

"No risk for a woman, Hogan."

Hogan's bright blue eyes sharpened. He nodded.

"You've got to consider all the possibilities. That's where you start—finding out who saw who, coming or going through any of these entrances."

He turned to me. "You were sitting facing this room, Mrs. Latham. Did you see anyone come in here, or come out?"

I saw Clem Bonner move again. I knew instantly, of course, what was in his mind . . . and also that there was nothing for it.

"My niece came in here during dinner, and stayed a few minutes," I said. "She certainly didn't have a rope with her. And I doubt if she could tie a knot to save her life."

Hogan grunted. "Didn't need to. Anybody could jerk a noose and loop a rope around a pedestal. Get her in."

He nodded to one of his men. I didn't dare look at Clem.

Judy came swiftly through the doors, her face pale, her eyes steady and unflinching.

"Nobody was in here when I was," she said. "Except that a man—I thought one of the waiters—looked in through some kind of a hole in that wall."

She pointed to the panel opening into the passage to the kitchen and alley.

"You know who it was?"

"I'm not sure. I think it was the man Sergeant Buck brought back. Not Whitey—the other one."

"Vicki wasn't here?"

"No. I was only here a couple of minutes. I went out through the powder room there. Nobody was there but Mrs. de Courcey. I didn't see Vicki at all, not after she came in with you, Colonel Primrose."

Colonel Primrose nodded. "You can go, Mrs. Bonner. Ask Mrs. de Courcey to come in, Buck.—Wait a minute."

He turned to me. "Who is that girl with Judy?"

"That's Polly Wagner," I said.

He nodded to Buck, and in a minute Polly Wagner came in . . . Polly with her charming simple sanity, and the sort of incandescent glow of hope behind her clear eyes that still almost redeems Reno in spite of everything . . . the gambling, and the dope, and the general vulgarity.

"Yes, I saw Judy come out here," she said. "But she wasn't here long. She just came out because she couldn't sit there another minute and have somebody looking like a hungry brook trout across the room, never taking his eyes off her."

She gave Clem a quick amused glance.

"I mean, she couldn't possibly, because—odd as it may seem—she's really perfectly mad about him."

I thought her disarming smile softened even the monolithic visage of Sergeant Buck.

"But that's not what you're interested in, is it. I know she was just here a minute or so. And I wasn't even paying the least attention to anybody else. The man I was talking to has fifteen thousand sheep up on the range, and we were talking about them, and he's down here to get a doctor to take up with him tomorrow because his Basque herder's got a sick wife.—The only odd thing I noticed was that Vicki—I don't know her as well as people who live in town do—seemed sort of excited . . . like people do when they're . . . oh, taking a ski jump and aren't sure whether they're going to land or break their necks."

Colonel Primrose nodded, looking rather curiously at her. "I . . . thought so too," he said. "All right, Mrs. Wagner." He nodded to Buck.

Mary de Courcey had on a black chiffon dress and a tight fitting black crownless turban over her flaming red hair, and —a little to my surprise—she was dreadfully upset.

"Oh, that poor girl!" she whispered. "It's *horrible!*"

She kept her eyes away from the table. I was surprised still more to see that they were suddenly filled with tears.

"Mrs. Bonner says she saw you in the powder room, Mary," Colonel Primrose said quietly.

"Yes, of course. Why shouldn't she?"

Mrs. de Courcey wiped her eyes and resumed her crisp and masterful manner.

"She came out here, out of this room. We talked a minute —I don't remember what about—and she went on through the powder room. Vicki came in while I was still there. I was repairing a shoulder-strap, if it interests you. She helped me, and I went back to the bar."

"Leaving Vicki there?"

"Yes. She'd flopped down in a chair and lighted a cigarette. She'd been in to see me late this afternoon, she had a rambling story about people perjuring themselves, or something —I didn't make head or tail of it. She wanted to know what happened to them, and all that."

I looked at her, remembering her voice coming out of the room as I stood in the hall watching Judy go down to the elevator: "That's nothing but blackmail!" As I turned away my eyes caught Colonel Primrose's. He was looking at me intently.

He turned back at once to Mrs. de Courcey. Her blue eyes were fastened, for the first time, on the lace folds of Vicki's dress.

"John!" she said abruptly. "This doesn't make sense! No one would want to hurt that girl. Whatever they say about her—and it's plenty, and it's all true—she was one of the most amusing, and generous, and kindhearted people I've ever met in all my life. She really was! Believe me, I can't think anybody would want to . . . to kill her."

She twisted her hands together, agitated and distressed and I thought really hurt.

"I don't suppose it makes the least sense, and I'm certainly the last person in the world—"

She stopped abruptly.

"What is it, Mary?"

An odd look came into Mrs. de Courcey's handsome face.

"You know I'm not likely to start pretending I'm psychic at my age, John," she said slowly, her manner quite different from any I'd noticed in her. "But when I was out at the bar, and Mrs. Latham here screamed 'It's Kaye Gorman!' . . . I . . . I just knew it was right—that Kaye Gorman was dead. I knew it—even though I could see her in the mirror. It was like Dracula, John, only just the opposite—you know the man couldn't see Dracula in the mirror, and a mirror was just where I *was* seeing her, but I knew that even if I could see her in the mirror I couldn't ever see her in the flesh again!"

Bill Hogan looked oddly at Colonel Primrose. "That's screwy, ma'am," he said.

"Exactly!" Mrs. de Courcey cried. "It's completely screwy! But there it is! I suppose all it means is that I wasn't at all surprised to hear something appalling had happened to Mrs. Gorman—as if I'd been expecting it. And yet it hadn't! And I think the reason Mrs. Gorman looked so frightened was that she was thinking exactly the same thing!"

Hogan scowled. I sympathized with him, entirely.

A light flickered in Colonel Primrose's eyes. I took it he'd made some sense out of it.

"They were both wearing black lace dresses," he said.

Hogan looked at him. "One of you boys get Mrs. Gorman in here," he said curtly.

Mary de Courcey followed the man out.

"If somebody had to be dead every time some woman started screaming her head off," Sergeant Buck said harshly, out of one corner of his granite jaw, "the town would look like a slaughterhouse."

He gave me a fishy glance. "No offense meant, ma'am."

"None taken, Sergeant," I said, sweetly. I resisted a strong temptation to add, "You big tomato!" in the language of my younger son. Reno was really the perfect spot for most of his speech.

A sudden confused babble rose from the bar as Kaye Gorman came through the doors.

"Mrs. Gorman," Colonel Primrose said, "—we're trying to find out who was in the powder room this evening. Did you see anyone in there, coming or going?"

As she lifted those baby-blue eyes to him I had the sudden thought that I personally would never believe a word she said.

"I was in there once, Colonel. I was washing my hands in the little back room. I heard somebody come in, but there was nobody there when I came out."

"When did you see Vicki last? Do you remember?"

"No, I don't. You know the way she went in and out. I don't think I saw her after the orchestra came in. She took that rope from somebody and said 'You'd better let me check that, cowboy.' Somebody at the bar said 'You don't need rope to throw 'em, Vicki.' I don't know who it was. I guess it sounded funny, because we all laughed fit to kill."

She turned away, her lips quivering suddenly. "The poor kid, it's a damn shame! But I guess it shows she didn't kill Dex."

She looked at me.

Colonel Primrose, whose eyes had been fixed absently on the black lace folds of her dinner dress and her silver kid sandals, looked at her, and at me.

"Has anyone said she did, Mrs. Gorman?"

She raised her eyes to his, round and blue as delft saucers.

"I don't mean they've actually been accusing her. But you know how there's always a lot of talk around the bars."

Clem Bonner, standing there by the window, moved suddenly again. In the glare of the lights that Hogan's men had brought in I could see his face flushing. I wondered what he was thinking, and whether what he had told me, about himself and Kaye Gorman, was true . . . not doubting it, exactly, even in face of Judy's seeing her go into his room, but wondering, nevertheless.

And I looked at Kaye Gorman, wondering if what Colonel Primrose obviously had in mind—that Vicki had been attacked by mistake, the murderer thinking from the black lace dress that she was Kaye—made any sense. Kaye Gorman did not look like my idea of a *femme fatale*. Vicki had been more like it, some way, with that slow and secret smile of hers.

21

Colonel Primrose's black eyes rested on Kaye Gorman's blue eyes with a kind of placid but steady wariness.

"I see," he said. "By the way, Mrs. Gorman, didn't you tell Mr. Hogan here that you went to bed early—around one-thirty o'clock—Monday night, when Cromwell was killed?"

"Yes. I told him that. I did go to bed early. I don't know whether it was one or not, but it wasn't two. Dex brought me home from here. I was a little vague about time. You know how it is after you've met a lot of old friends and had a drink with each of them."

There was no change in her hard voice, but she smiled a little.

Colonel Primrose did not smile. "You weren't present, then, when Mr. Bonner here had his little set-to with Cromwell?"

A sharp note came into her voice instantly.

"No—I wasn't! Does anybody say I was?"

She looked angrily at Clem.

"I didn't say you were," Clem said quietly.

She laughed her short laugh.

"Well, I hope not! I mean, after all—we were friends, once . . ."

Clem said nothing.

"All right, Mrs. Gorman," Colonel Primrose said. "And by the way, Bonner," he went on after she'd gone out, "when did you see Miss Ray last?"

"I saw her take that rope," Clem said quietly. "As Mrs. Gorman did. Furthermore, I saw her go into the powder room . . . with the rope in her hand."

Colonel Primrose nodded, looking steadily at him. "I wondered if she didn't," he said. "You're sure of that?"

Clem nodded.

"She'd been talking to a fellow who was showing her how to handle it."

"When was that?"

Clem hesitated, and turned to me. "It was before Polly finished her dinner, Grace. I mean, she was still at your table."

He grinned suddenly, without much mirth.

"I was sitting there, thinking I wished she'd quit looking so damned much like she was looking through the gates of Heaven, or something . . . and thinking that's the way Judy used to look, before . . . oh, well."

Colonel Primrose looked at me with a faint smile in his eyes.

"You didn't go out of the room yourself?"

"Yes, I did. I went out to look at Frenchy's wine cellar and the new kitchens."

"After you saw Vicki go in the powder room with the rope?" Hogan asked sharply.

"Yes. Just after. The little fellow they call Whitey asked me if I didn't want to see them. He said 'We got great pride in this joint.' That's why I went. I didn't want to see the damn things."

"Whitey was with you all the time you were out?"

"Yes.—Well, no. Not exactly. I mean, I was talking to the chef. He used to work at Mori's on 56th Street. We had a drink out there, just the two of us. Whitey wasn't there then. We went out together, and he was next to me at the bar when Mrs. Latham screamed."

"He could possibly have had time to come in this room?"

Clem nodded slowly. "I think so. I'm not saying he did, or even that I saw him leave. He just wasn't there in the kitchen when the chef and I had that drink."

"And about Monday night, Mr. Bonner," Colonel Primrose said placidly. "You told Mr. Wilstack you got off the night plane, registered, under an assumed name, at the Washoe, and didn't leave your room until you went to Mrs. Bonner's room.—Do you want to amend that?"

"No."

"Then when was it you saw Cromwell?"

Clem grinned down at me—still not mirthfully.

"I didn't say I saw him."

"You did see him, however."

"How do you know?"

"Your fingerprints are on his car—gripping the left door, by the wheel, with both hands. It also has certain streaks just by them that apparently show your hands being jerked off—as if the car was started suddenly while you were still hanging on.—That's correct, isn't it?"

Clem's voice was hard and wary. "What if it is?"

I could see that Colonel Primrose was counting ten, or something, just as I'd done so many times with Judy.

"It bears on what happened—about your wife, Bonner—the night Cromwell was killed.—Did you take that candle pick from her table during your argument with her? Had somebody already got it? Did somebody come in later and get it? Did nobody get it at all—was it used by Judith Bonner and no one else? What you did bears on all those things.—You see, Bonner, the general idea is that somebody went out to the race track with Cromwell . . . or followed him out there because someone else was already in the car with him . . ."

Clem shook his head curtly.

"If you mean I followed him out there because my wife was in the car with him, you're dead wrong."

"She wasn't in the car?"

"She wasn't."

"Who was in the car?"

"Cromwell—nobody else."

"Is that a fact, Bonner?"

"Yes."

They looked at each other steadily a long moment. I knew, and therefore Colonel Primrose must have known, that Clem was not telling the truth. A curious light flickered in Colonel Primrose's eyes, as if he was hearing something that was terribly important.

"Did your meeting with Cromwell come before, or after, your session with your wife?"

"Before," Clem said quietly.

"I suppose there's no point in asking what you talked about?"

"Right. It's . . . obvious."

"Or what you and Miss Ray talked about this afternoon? —I'm told she visited you around one o'clock. Correct?"

"Right."

"How long have you known Miss Ray?"

"Since around one o'clock," Clem said coolly.

One of Bill Hogan's men came in and handed Hogan a list of names. "That's the lot," he said. "Everybody that was here."

Hogan passed the list to Colonel Primrose, who checked several names on it and handed it back. "Clear everybody else out," he said. He looked at me. "You might take Mrs. Bonner back to the hotel. And I'd like to see her in the morning."

I didn't see who stayed, in the mad scramble of nearly everybody to get out of the River House. Judy and Polly Wagner were already near the door, talking to the white-haired old man who came in to play the piano for an hour each evening for his food. And anyway I was so relieved that we were let off for once that my curiosity was momentarily in abeyance. We hurried along to Virginia Street and across the bridge.

A crowd of girls from Polly's ranch were waiting for her in the cocktail lounge. She joined them, Judy and I stopped at the desk for her key.

"You've got both keys out, Mrs. Bonner," the night clerk said, turning from the empty pigeon hole under her room number. "Here's Mrs. Latham's key."

We went up and through my room to Judy's sitting room. Her key was on the table. She picked it up and looked at it for a moment. Then she turned to me, a puzzled look in her serious gray eyes.

"Grace—didn't I give my other key to Dex, Monday night, to come up and get my jacket?"

I nodded . . . the thought never entering my tired and numbed mind of how terribly important that could be.

She walked over to the window and drew the curtains together. She turned back slowly.

"You know, Grace, I keep telling myself I must be developing a persecution complex," she said, with an attempt at a smile.

"Why, darling?" I said.

"Because the more I think of it, the less I can help think somebody's really trying to make the police think I killed Dex."

"It was bound to dawn on you sooner or later, darling," I said. "Everybody else has had that unpleasant idea for a long time now."

She looked at me with gray bewildered eyes, her oval face under her golden hair a pale inscrutable mask that belied her next remark.

"I'm beginning to be absolutely terrified. Mr. Martin went over all the evidence against me this morning.—I suddenly had the wild idea that maybe I did do it. And now . . . Vicki. Wait till they find out that Joe Lucas has taught me a lot of parlor tricks with a lariat."

She stopped abruptly, and went, as if she had just remembered something, to the desk there. She opened the drawer and riffled through the note paper, her hands a little unsteady.

"I burned the sample letter, darling," I said.

She drew a deep breath.

"That's a break," she said coolly.

"—Unless you finished a copy including all its worst features, and it's still floating around."

She nodded, and gave me a quick little smile.

"I did. That's what I went up to Tahoe for the other night. Not that it matters."

She came and sat down by me. "It wouldn't matter, anyway, except that I shouldn't have mentioned anybody's name. That was stupid. But I . . . I just didn't like the way Dex was playing up to Mrs. de Courcey. It wasn't because I was jealous—I already knew I'd never marry him, after I'd got my . . . divorce. You see, she's got a pretty big settlement from General de Courcey, and both Whitey and this Ewing were trying to get money out of her. And I almost begin to think Dex was too. I guess that's a foul thing to say, but I think he was."

"Don't you think," I remarked dryly, "that Mrs. de Courcey is quite old enough to take care of herself?"

She shook her head.

"Anywhere else, maybe. Not out here. Everything's so plausible and . . . and open, in Reno, that it's terribly hard to see it's all just part of an enormous build-up to get your money.—I loaned Whitey a hundred and fifty dollars to pay his mother's hospital bill, and Dex made him give it back to me—his mother's been dead fifteen years."

She smiled. I couldn't help thinking about Dex's mother. It had worked the other way, in her case.

"What about Vicki?" I asked. "Did she collect money from people too?"

Judy shrugged.

"Mrs. de Courcey probably gave her some. I know she gave her clothes. But only because she was really fond of her."

I heard the door across the hall open and close, and almost

immediately open and close again. There was a knock at Judy's door, and Mrs. de Courcey came in as soon as we'd got it unlocked.

22

"My dears, I'm worn out!" she said. "I can't bear to stay in there by myself. May I come in?"

"Of course," Judy said.

Mrs. de Courcey lighted a cigarette. She was nervous and jumpy and kept taking out her vanity and putting rouge on her cheeks, as if she saw a pallor there that no one else could see.

"I suppose you were talking about Vicki—it's too awful."

She turned abruptly to Judy.

"Were you here this afternoon about two?"

Judy glanced at me. "Around then. Why?"

"I was just wondering," Mrs. de Courcey said. "Wondering if anyone might have overheard a talk she and I were having. It didn't make sense to me, but if anybody had heard it who could make sense out of it, then all this might be a little more understandable."

I stared quite openly at her merry, handsome, commanding face under that marvellous henna hair, wondering myself if what she was now telling us made any sense.

She hesitated a moment. Then she said, quite abandoning her mannered garrulity for the second time since I'd known her, "It was that idea of being overheard that made me think of those little doors where you set the garbage tins in. They're quite big enough for anybody to open and listen through—easily."

I still stared, wondering if she was only trying to find out if she and Vicki Ray had been overheard, or was trying to say something and finding it difficult to say.

"In fact, if you're small enough you can even get through them.—I couldn't, of course, but Whitey did, one afternoon when I left my keys inside."

She looked intently, and rather oddly, at Judy.

"In fact, my dear, I've been wondering if somebody got into your apartment that way, and put that candle holder arrangement in your hamper, to make it look as if . . ."

She waved her cigarette to indicate the rest of her meaning.

"I'm awfully interested in all this, of course—apart from you, I mean, Judy . . . and it's perfectly absurd of them to think for a minute that you did it.—You won't believe me, but they've had the police asking questions about me. The General's in a stew—he's afraid if I get involved in a scandal I won't get a divorce."

There was something very startling in the complete disillusionment in her voice. I looked at her in surprise. The manner had completely disappeared. She'd slumped against the cushions, all the crisp merriment in her eyes gone. She was suddenly nothing but a tired old woman, whose mask of gaiety and bright sophistication had dropped and broken at our feet.

"My husband's retiring next month," she said abruptly. "He's wanted to marry . . . somebody for five years. But he couldn't, not while he was in the Service. We had to keep face, so we went on. It's funny . . . to find yourself not needed any more—even for appearances."

She got up, went over to the cocktail bar and poured herself a Scotch and soda mechanically, not, I'm sure, even aware that she wasn't in her own apartment.

"I think that's why so many of us who come out here go so completely berserk, and take up with people we'd never know existed, if it weren't for the movies. The most extraordinary things seem normal here. I've loaned people money I know I'll never see again, on hard luck stories that wouldn't have deceived a babe in New York."

She drained her glass. Judy and I watched her move aimlessly around the room. I still have no idea whether she was on the point of saying something else. There was something on her mind, obviously.

She stopped at the windows and drew the curtains apart.

"I never think what a cesspool Reno is, until I look up at the sky at night," she said abruptly. "Then people like Frenchy, and Whitey . . ."

She shrugged her shoulders.

"All of them . . . scrabbling around, sly and tricky, selling a three-dollar dinner for a dollar and a half as a come-on for their crooked gambling tables. Definitely like something you'd find under a board in a cellar. If it weren't for the nights, serene and star-studded, I couldn't stick it."

She stepped out onto the balcony. Neither Judy nor I said anything. After a moment I saw her glance to the right, and stiffen perceptibly. She came back into the room.

"That's odd," she said. "I understood Mr. Ewing was too . . . too ill to be out. I understand from Whitey, by the way, that he's not getting a divorce at all. He's an artist, of some kind."

Judy glanced at me, her deep fringed gray eyes lighting in the first sudden spontaneous and mirthful smile I'd seen in them since I came to Reno.

"I suppose," Mrs. de Courcey said, "that's why he doesn't seem popular with the men. Though Dex liked him. He was the only one who seemed to. You remember, Judy, he was up at his place at Tahoe quite frequently, you've probably seen him there."

A tiny surprised question darted through Judy's eyes.

"I wasn't ever up there but once, in the morning for a minute, to pick Dex up when his car was in the garage."

"He used to come with Vicki and Joe Lucas, in Joe's car," Mrs. de Courcey said. "He must have money. He certainly dressed well, and I certainly saw him lose six hundred dollars downstairs one night."

She flicked her cigarette into the empty fireplace.

"Well, I'd better let you people go to bed. You both look completely fagged. Good night."

She closed the door behind her.

I felt she wasn't thinking about either of us then, actually, and I was sure of it when I didn't hear her door open and close . . . not for some time after I'd gone to bed. I lay there, quite sleepless, thinking about Vicki Ray . . . wondering grotesquely if she had greeted the dark ferryman with her same breezy salute and her slow secret smile as she stepped into his grim stone boat to cross the river of Death.

That sentence spoken in the River House—"Whatever they say about her, and it's plenty, and it's all true, she was one of the most amusing, and generous, and kindhearted people"—came into my mind again as I heard Mrs. de Courcey's key in her door, and the door closing very quietly. I wondered again who had told Mrs. de Courcey that Dexter Cromwell was dead, that night, before she came into Judy's apartment.

23

I've wondered a number of times what actual difference it might have made in what happened later if I hadn't been standing at the desk reading my mail when Clem Bonner stepped out of the elevator the next morning, or even if the desk clerk hadn't said, at precisely the moment he was heading toward the door, "Mrs. Bonner's car has come, Mrs. Latham."

He stopped, crossed the lobby and came over to me.

"Hello," he said. "Where are you going?"

"Nowhere in particular," I said. "I just thought I'd drive out in the great open spaces and take a look at the desert."

He hesitated. "Do you think Judy would mind if you drove me up to Lake Tahoe?"

"What for?" I asked.

"Nothing. I've just got to go, that's all."

That's how I went. He took the wheel, and grinned suddenly. "She won't let me drive her car, at home."

"Men ruin cars," I said. "That's one of the things every woman knows."

I glanced at him there, hatless in the sun. He'd aged during this, I thought. Not that his hair had turned white, but his face was firmer, and harder, his eyes sombre, with a deep aching hunger in them that he couldn't hide. He looked more as if he knew better now what it was he wanted, and would be a little hard to stop when he decided to get it.

We went out Virginia Street, past the road to the airport where I'd come in Monday evening, leaving behind us the hot dog and doughnut and fruit stands and the tourist camps, past the lovely big cottonwood tree on the left before the road turns off for Virginia City, and turned right near the hot springs into the mountain road. The sun burned on the yellow sage and the gray sand and the paper-white blooms of the desert primrose lining the road, and the purple lupin spreading its small bright carpet here and there. Ring-necked squirrels as gray-dun as the sand scampered across in front of us, and above us loomed Mount Rose, still capped with winter snow.

The road was very steep after we left the flat hot desert and began climbing—pitted from frost and covered with gravel washed down the banks with the melting snows. Very suddenly we came out of the few scrubby aspens and pines, and rounded a sharp curve from which the universe seemed to fall abruptly away, leaving us looking far down on the Washoe meadows, lying sun-bathed between the two dun-colored ridges, tiny and domestic and far away. We were looking out on chasms of rock . . . edges drear and naked shingles of the world.

The car skidded crazily in the gravel. I grabbed the door. Clem grinned, and I tried to, but my hands were quite cold with sudden fright. Looking back on it now, I have a quite irrational notion that that was nothing more or less than some kind of a foreshadowing . . . of what that steep narrow winding road was to mean, of the horror that it was to hold for all of us.

He threw the car into second and kept close to the bank except where the rocks were in the way. I fastened my eyes on the road, trying not to look at the vast fortresses of stone far under us. We reached the plateau finally, where great patches of snow lay among the flower-carpeted knolls, and it was cold in spite of the burning sun, and the air was like sparkling burgundy, rich and tangy; and suddenly we saw the ribbon of cobalt below us through the trees, where Lake Tahoe lay, bluer than the Mediterranean. We began to go down, in second again till we came to the last stretch before the road that runs around the lake.

Clem hadn't spoken since we'd left the road through the Washoe meadows. As we turned right along the lake he said, "I had a talk with Judy last night, after you went to bed."

I waited.

"Maybe she wasn't as goofy about Cromwell as I thought," he went on, after some time.

"She's . . . still going on with the divorce?"

I sounded exactly like a Reno lawyer about to lose a client through an unfortunate reconciliation.

He nodded. "I . . . couldn't ask her not to," he said. "It wouldn't be fair . . . not when all this has got her down."

I looked at him.

"Which seems pretty stupid to me," I said tartly. "If it's got her down, it's just when she needs you. But it hadn't occurred to me . . . I mean, I thought she was bearing up amazingly. It's my chief reason for believing she didn't actually care a snap for Dexter Cromwell—except out of a sort of wounded heart that would clutch at anything."

He didn't say anything. His eyes were fastened on the road, his hands gripped the wheel harder.

"I mean," I said, "that I think you're being preternaturally blind."

A dark flush crept up his cheek. We drove on in silence. After a minute or so we came to an enormous building set down on the lake shore that looked like a cross between a rustic cathedral and an alpine shooting lodge.

"That's the place where the dance floor has the state line marked across it," he said moodily. "The divorcées scurry across it at midnight to keep on the Nevada side. Just more of the Reno clowning."

We passed that, and the young men looking for boll weevils, or Japanese beetles, or something, and turned in, not very far along, through a rustic gate set between two towering pines.

"Would this be where Cromwell lived?" I asked.

He nodded.

"I do hope we've got a jolly good reason for coming here, then," I said frostily. "—Just in case anyone happens to be here to ask."

"Don't worry," he said curtly. "There'll be a China boy. He goes with the place."

I had just started to ask him how he knew so much about it when he pulled up beside an empty corral and put on the brakes. Through the trees I could see a green lawn, and great spikes of delphinium against the gleaming white stucco of a little turreted chalet, and beyond it the glimmering sapphire of the lake.

The dead pine needles made a noiseless carpet for our feet as we went along to the terrace and crossed it. The door was open a little. We went in—Clem very much as if he knew what he was doing, and myself more than a little dubious. I stopped just inside the door. We were in a pine-panelled room with white bearskin rugs and soft red leather furniture. Clem crossed the room. I watched him uneasily. He didn't tip-toe, but he kept on the rugs when he might have clattered on the pine floor if he hadn't.

At the side of the fireplace across from the door we'd come in by, he fumbled at what looked like a quite ordinary small panel, and slid it back into the wall. I saw then that it was the door of a liquor closet that ran through to the other side, like a buttery opening into the kitchen. There were glasses and decanters and a couple of half-empty bottles in there. As I stood waiting by the door, quite motionless and not liking this in the least, Clem quietly lifted a small mahogany box off a shelf to his right in the side of the closet, put it down in front of him, opened it, stood looking down into it for a moment, started to close it and stopped, every muscle abruptly tensed.

He turned silently and held up his hand as I started to speak. I could hear the voices coming through the panel closet then, and I crept toward Clem, on the white bearskin rugs. The door at the other end of the concealed cupboard was closed, but I could hear the singsong tones of the China boy, and another voice that I knew well. I started to move away, my heart beating violently. Clem caught my wrist and held it.

Colonel Primrose was saying, "All right, Wu Lung. Just see if you can tell us if any of these people used to visit Mr. Cromwell."

The China boy's voice was high and cheerful.

"Velly okay. Wu Lung she never forget anybody face. Missy he allays say Wu Lung she never forget anybody face, ever."

"Then look at these," Colonel Primrose said patiently.

I could hear the ruffle of stiff polished paper, and that high, amused, polite voice: "Oh, see!" . . . as if Wu Lung had pounced forward with joy and recognition and helpfulness.

And then—and never could I have believed it for an instant if I had not heard it with my own ears—: *"He Missy Bonner . . . he all time stay week-end with Clomwell!"*

I stood there, for an interminable moment, paralyzed beyond any sensation at all, unable to think or to feel . . . and above all to realize, consciously, that I had heard that incredible, damning statement, so cheerful and so dreadful, and at the same time so straightforward.

I was almost unconscious of Clem's fingers tightening on my wrist so that they were almost breaking it. I looked slowly around at him. His face was quite white, under his heavy tan, for a moment; then the blood rushed darkly into his cheeks. He let go my wrist, and stood there, stunned, just looking down.

Through the fog in my brain I heard the high sing-song voice.

"That Whitey. She all time come. She all time dlunk.— That Joe Cowboy. She come one two thlee time. She all time tell Clomwell she talk too much.—Missy Cou'cey, he all time here.—Missy Vicki, he not all time here, he all time telephone.—No . . . he not here.—No. No."

I could see one photograph after another bringing no recognition. Wu Lung was still saying "No . . . she not here," when Clem Bonner quietly closed the panel, turned without a word or sign, crossed the room quietly and went out. I followed. We got in the car, neither of us saying a word. The car moved silently on the pine needle carpet. Out on the road he gripped the wheel and put his foot down. We went along maniacally, the needle swinging dizzily at seventy-five, Clem's face that of a man who had taken a sip of nectar and found it corroding acid . . . more terribly hurt than I would have thought it was possible for him to be.

I sat there, hanging on to the door as we lurched savagely around curves, trying desperately to think of something to say that wouldn't sound cruelly banal . . . hurt terribly myself, unbelieving, and yet bound to believe. I couldn't think of a thing, so I didn't say anything.

He jammed the brakes on suddenly and drew up at an inn along the road.

"You go on back, will you?" he said quietly. "I'll be along later."

He got out and slammed the door shut. I moved over under the wheel, still too distressed and too upset to think or speak coherently. I just stared blindly at him.

He gave me a twisted sardonic smile.

"I guess we were both wrong," he said. "So long."

He went deliberately through the swinging doors of the inn bar as if they hadn't been there. The doors swung violently back. I sat there staring stupidly after him. I don't know how long I stayed there, but it must have been some time. A car, coming along at about the speed we'd been making, drew up sharply at the gas pump with a screech of brakes, and Sergeant Buck got out—his grim face solider granite and fishier-eyed as he spotted me. He picked up the water can and unscrewed the radiator cap.

Their car door opened again almost immediately, and Colonel Primrose came over to where I was sitting, my hand on the gear shift, my foot still motionless on the clutch.

"What are you doing up here?" he asked quickly. His eyes were probing, and worried.

"I . . . just came for the ride," I said, making what must have been a pitiful effort to be casual.

"Then you go on back, at once," he said. He was looking intently at me. "Listen . . . carefully," he said. "There's a killer around here—coldblooded, desperate, still at large. You could easily be in terrible danger.—I don't want you off anywhere by yourself."

He stopped, still looking intently at me. "—Do you know who killed Cromwell, and Vicki Ray?"

"No," I said blankly. "I don't. Should I?"

"You've never accused anybody, or expressed any opinion that any particular person did it?"

"No," I said. "Don't be ridiculous. Of course I haven't."

I didn't realize, in the remotest degree, how mistaken that was . . . or how near it came to being fatally mistaken.

His face cleared.

"I . . . do know," he said. "The case is broken—as soon as we get a couple of loose ends tied up. You go on back, and don't stop on the way, and stay in the Washoe bar, or some place with other people.—Have you any idea where Clem Bonner is?"

"Not the foggiest, Colonel Primrose," I said.

He nodded and went back to his car. There was a kind of stony triumph in the otherwise dead pan of Sergeant Phineas

T. Buck as he brought the water can back. It was nothing to
the triumph in my own face as I waited till they'd disappeared and went into the bar there to tell Clem Bonner
that if he was planning to go on a bender, he'd better wait
till it would be rather simpler to explain.

24

The clerk beckoned to me very discreetly as Clem and I came
into the lobby of the Washoe an hour later. I went across to
the desk.

"The police were here asking about Mrs. Bonner's car,
Mrs. Latham."

He glanced to the right and left to see that we weren't being overheard.

"I said you had it up at Tahoe. They said to ask you to
bring it around to the station when you came, if you didn't
mind."

I suppose I looked disturbed in spite of myself, for
he added reassuringly, "I'm very confident everything's quite
all right, Mrs. Latham. But I did take the liberty of not mentioning it to Mrs. Bonner when she went out."

He turned to my room box and brought out a couple of
phone call slips and my key and handed them to me.

"Mrs. Bonner went out with the young lady from Sun
Mountain Ranch—Mrs. Wagner, I believe? They were going out there to ride."

I said "Thanks very much," and went back out into the
sun-baked street, thinking how extraordinarily *au fait* the
clerk at the Washoe was with his guests' goings and comings.
I was thinking too that it was amusing how perfectly at ease
I was when I knew those two were together. Murder, divorce,
dope, gambling, racketeering . . . nothing could defile Polly
Wagner's high sanity, or Judy's, now that she was coming
back to herself again.

I stopped just outside the hotel doors to put on my dark
glasses against the blinding white glare, and heard someone
rapping vigorously on the window of the cocktail lounge.

I turned around. Whitey and Kaye Gorman and Cowboy
Joe were there, motioning me to come in. I shook my head
and pointed across the Truckee. Whitey raised the window
and thrust a slightly battered ear out.

"How's that?"

"I can't," I said. "I'm going to the police station."

He waggled his head in disgust.

I went on to the car, parked it in front of the entrance to the Y. W. C. A., which always seemed curiously out of place under the police station, and went up the stairs. The desk sergeant took his feet down off a table hastily and got up.

"Right through there, lady," he said.

I went through the inner room. A couple of men, hangdog and furtive, sat twirling their caps between their knees. There was also a man there not so hangdog, his head bandaged and his face—what showed of it—purple and black and yellow. He gave me a malignant glare out of swollen eyes. I had suspected that Mr. Steve Ewing would not care much for me after what had happened to him, but I hadn't, some way, thought of him as a continuing menace. I went on into the sunny room with its filing cabinets and broad desks and the Bertillon stand against the wall with the small American flag stuck at the top. Bill Hogan was fingerprinting a boy who couldn't have been older than my older one. They'd picked him up, I learned, trying to change a capful of quarters at a service station out the Truckee . . . which around these parts always meant a broken slot machine somewhere.

The boy went out, Colonel Primrose came in with a young man in a white work overall with the name of a garage sewed in red thread across the back. Colonel Primrose gave me a half-annoyed half-quizzical look and shook his head. I gathered he'd heard I came back with Clem.

"Did you bring the car?" he asked.

I nodded. "It's out in front."

Bill Hogan motioned to the garage man. They both leaned over the desk and looked out the window.

"That's it all right. I ain't making any mistake."

I glanced from the two of them to Colonel Primrose, not understanding.

"I've been away on my vacation, or I'd been in sooner," the man said.

"You took it out to Clinton Street?"

The man nodded.

"I picked it up like I do every night when it's standing in front of the hotel after midnight, and took it in. That was about half-past twelve. About one-thirty Mrs. Bonner called up, and said she was walking home from a party, and would I mind taking the car out to the saloon on Fourth Street and Clinton and leave it there for her. Would I leave the keys in the usual place—we always leave 'em under the rubber floor mat if they don't have an extra one, and she'd come off without hers—and take a taxi back and charge it to her. She's always swell to work with, which most of 'em out here for the cure ain't.—So I did, and then I picked it up again in Island Street near the hotel, about three."

I looked at Colonel Primrose, still in the completest bewilderment.

"I asked her was anything wrong. She said no, everybody was having a lot of drink and she'd rather be in her own car doing the driving herself, which I didn't blame her at all, the way some of these palookas drink. So, I took it out and left it."

Colonel Primrose nodded.

"You're sure it was Mrs. Bonner that phoned you?"

He spoke pleasantly, but I could hear the tenseness in his voice.

"Oh, sure."

Bill Hogan moved uncomfortably.

"There's no getting away from that, Colonel," he said, as if he would very much have liked to get away from it if he could. "The girl at the switchboard put in the call to the garage for her at half-past one."

Colonel Primrose shook his head.

"*No,*" he said. "I don't believe it. I'm telling you it's all wrong. Too many things are supposed to have happened in Mrs. Bonner's room. It's too much, Hogan. That weapon was in her room, it was taken from her room, it was found in her room, wrapped in her riding shirt, in her clothes hamper. And now a call for her car is put in from her room."

He pointed down to a manila envelope on the desk.

"And all the time we have got there those hairs from Mrs. Bonner's head that were taken from the hand of the murdered man, on the wheel of that car."

Bill Hogan pulled the envelope toward him. It had "Coroner" printed on it in big black letters. He opened it and took out a long slide. I could see those bright red-gold hairs mounted in it. I have never known less what to think or what to do in my whole life.

Colonel Primrose didn't look at me.

"Without those hairs," he went on quietly, "what Mr. Nelson here says would be just about enough to convict Mrs. Bonner.—With them, it is absolutely impossible that she could have committed this crime."

My head swam round in dizzy circles. Bill Hogan gave the impression of a man nodding his head and shaking it at the same time . . . wanting to believe, and unable to.

"It's conceivable, though highly improbable, that Mrs.

Bonner—assuming she murdered Cromwell—would have taken a shirt out with her to wrap up her grisly relic, brought it back to her room and stuck it in her clothes hamper, when it would have been perfectly simple to leave it out there . . . or, if she'd brought it back, to wash it off under the tap and stick it up on the mantel, and just maintain it was never out of her room. You know there are hundreds of those things about—and Mrs. Bonner must have known it if she'd been in that museum and curiosity shop at Virginia City."

He tapped the slide with a pencil.

"But this is absolutely incontrovertible proof that somebody is trying, desperately and with persistent cunning—too persistent to be terribly intelligent—to make it look as if Judy Bonner was in that car, and killed Cromwell. And this business of the car being called from her room is one straw too many—the camel's back was broken already."

I gave up trying to understand anything. It had seemed to me that whether they proved anything else or not, the one thing those bright hairs did prove was that Judy had been in the car when Dex Cromwell had died . . . however much I didn't want to believe it, however desperately I refused to go further.

"If she had planned at one-thirty," Colonel Primrose went on imperturbably, "to kill Cromwell an hour or so later, and knew she'd be wanting her car near the race track for her getaway, why didn't she take it out herself, earlier? Why didn't she use her own key? Why call from her own hotel room, pretending she was at a party that it would be perfectly easy to prove never existed, and leave the most damning trail of evidence, when she could have avoided it in the easiest possible way? To presume that either she, or her husband, for that matter, killed Cromwell in a fit of passion following a quarrel at three o'clock is definitely out . . . for Mr. Nelson's testimony shows clearly that this crime was under way by half-past one."

He did glance at me then, with an amused, or partly amused, half smile, and went on gravely.

"I understand why you're hesitating. But any jury would accept Mrs. Latham's testimony—and mine—that those hairs were there, in the dead man's hand. I think any jury would see that Mrs. Latham just had exactly the idea that the murderer was trying cunningly to give. I think any jury would understand that however impulsive—and even unintelligent —what she did was, it was actuated by a plain and good motive . . . the desire to protect a loved one."

My face was burning. It was also, I have no doubt, a study in bewilderment.

Bill Hogan turned to me, puzzled and disturbed.

"Mrs. Latham," he said, "do you recognize those hairs?"

"I . . . yes," I said. "I do.—If they're the ones somebody took out of the pocket of my riding shirt."

"They are," Colonel Primrose said suavely. "I took them out myself—Sergeant Buck witnessing—while you were down in the Washoe Bar."

25

I had a sudden most embarrassing picture of that large figure in the buckaroo costume, stony-visaged and fishy-eyed, in my bathroom. I should imagine—to say the least—that it's not at all military to shower bath powder and towels around the way I do.

Sergeant Buck stood motionless and frozen-faced by the door, not bothering to give any sign of corroboration. Obviously his colonel's word needed no bush . . . though the figure is certainly not very apt unless there's some particularly thorny and rock-ribbed shrub that I don't know about.

"And where did you get them, Mrs. Latham?" Hogan asked quietly.

I swallowed.

"I took them out of Cromwell's hand, on the steering wheel of the car, when Colonel Primrose went to call you," I said.

"Did they come out easily?"

I was more bewildered than ever.

"Not . . . terribly."

"They came," Colonel Primrose said quietly. "If they had really been clutched by his hand before rigor set in, they wouldn't have come. They would have broken off. However, I think that apart from that, your jury would accept my testimony that of those hairs in his hand, as I saw plainly the first thing, only two had a root showing. The roots of the others—which at first I assumed had got broken off some way—were turned in the other direction . . . toward the windshield. They were put under his hand, of course, by somebody who didn't notice that small detail.

"And even if your jury wouldn't accept that," he went on calmly, "they'd have to accept the report of the Federal Bureau of Investigation—that all those hairs were dead. They weren't pulled from Mrs. Bonner's head. They came out naturally. They were taken from her hair brush or her comb

. . . just as her candle pick was taken from her room and her soiled shirt from her clothes hamper. And all, undoubtedly, at the same time . . . at one-thirty, when that message was put through for her car."

I sat back weakly in my chair.

Hogan turned to the garage man. "You sure you recognized Mrs. Bonner's voice when the call came through?" he asked sharply.

Mr. Nelson hesitated.

"If she hadn't said she was Mrs. Bonner," Colonel Primrose said quietly, "would you have known it was she?"

There was a doubtful note in Mr. Nelson's voice. "I don't know, for sure, when you put it like that. I was figuring she was at a party, like she said. She was talking low . . . whispering. I guess she didn't want any of 'em——"

Bill Hogan and Colonel Primrose exchanged one glance.

"Hell," Hogan said, "why didn't you say so? Good God, if there's anything about crime everybody knows more about than fingerprints, it's that one whispering voice sounds just like another. You can't even tell what kind of a voice it is, if they're whispering. Man, if we put you on the witness stand, with even a tenth-rate lawyer cross-examining you, you couldn't get away with saying it was a woman, much less Mrs. Bonner."

He sat there for a while, staring silently down at his desk, after Mr. Nelson had been dismissed. He turned abruptly to Colonel Primrose.

"This puts a different face on things," he said curtly. He hesitated again. "I guess you're right, Colonel. Go on with it, will you? I'll be over to the Washoe in ten minutes."

He turned back, picked up a stack of papers and began sorting them. As I started to follow Colonel Primrose out I saw one that caught my eye. It was a radiogram. I couldn't possibly have read it, but I saw the signature: "de Courcey." I looked at Colonel Primrose, reflecting that friendships, apparently, were playing no part in this affair.

A policeman came into the middle room as we went through and said, "Okay, Ewing—you're next," and I heard some one say, "That bird's up for a good stretch for extortion," just as Mr. Hogan's door closed again . . . and that was the last I ever heard of Mr. Steve Ewing.

"I'll see you in fifteen minutes," Colonel Primrose said.

As I drew up in front of the Washoe I saw his car—Sergeant Buck's car, rather, as according to Colonel Primrose he's the economic royalist of the two, thanks to funds accumulated by means of well-known Army games and carefully invested in filling stations and streets of houses in

California—stop in front of the porticoed county court house across the street. Both of them went up the broad stairs and disappeared inside.

I went up to my room. Judy wasn't back yet. I went into her sitting room, sat down on the sofa and lighted a cigarette, thinking with an almost unbearable weariness of the strange business of her car, and of what Colonel Primrose had said over at police headquarters, and wondering if he had meant it, really . . . and if so, where were we then, and who did he think had killed Cromwell and Vicki Ray? I didn't dare to think about the point that ached in my heart, hurting more than any of that . . . the thing the China boy at the Tahoe cottage had said about Judy Bonner and Dex. Whatever the business of those bright hairs, that anyway was true, and there was no getting around it. And the fact that it had made no change, apparently, in Colonel Primrose's conviction of Judy's innocence—in the killing of Dex Cromwell—was just the more disturbing to me.

I tried painfully to think in some kind of an ordered way. That Judy Bonner had planned coldbloodedly to kill Cromwell, and after doing it had kept all the evidence where it was bound to do her the most harm, didn't make sense. And it made still less to think that Clem Bonner had done it. Much as he hated Cromwell, he was not likely, by any stretch of the imagination, to murder him and try to make Judy suffer for it.

It followed, then, that it had been done by someone else . . . and someone with a motive that was so far hidden. It followed also that it was a motive not hidden to Vicki Ray— for there could hardly be any doubt that she had known, and was killed because she knew. I thought suddenly of when I'd waited with the wan girl outside the courtroom, when Vicki was making an obvious start to call on her friend the District Attorney. Then I sat bolt upright as a sudden idea occurred to me. Why had her landlord, Mr. Tucker, been so obviously frightened out of his wits there?

I wondered vaguely if Colonel Primrose too would be following the black-and-gold finger to the District Attorney's office, and if Mr. Tucker would be there again, watching him.

I got up and stepped out onto the balcony above the Truckee, thinking about the miner's candle holder and the soiled riding shirt, and how they could have been got into Judy's room after Cromwell had been killed, and for that matter how someone could have got in there to put in that call to Mr. Nelson for her car, at one-thirty Tuesday morning . . . and thinking too that Mr. Steve Ewing's balcony was too far off for him to have scrambled over, unless Mr. Ewing had considerably more Tarzan blood in him than he'd appeared to have the last time I saw him.

Then I stopped short as a scene in the lobby the first night I came flashed into my mind: Judy handing Dexter Cromwell her key and asking him to go back to the third floor for her jacket. Unless he'd given her back that key when he joined us in the River House, and I hadn't seen him doing it, then it would still have been in his pocket when he was killed, and his murderer could have taken it from him . . .

I don't know how long I'd been standing out there on the balcony, thinking about that, looking absently down into the Truckee, when I heard a voice, frightened and hysterical. It was coming from the open window to my left, beyond the fire escape; and it was so sharpened and desperate that I scarcely recognized it at first, even though I couldn't have any doubt whose it was.

"But I was so hideously worried!" Mrs. de Courcey was crying. "You know what he's like, John! He hasn't a warm drop of blood in his body! I knew if he found I'd been giving anybody money, he'd hold up the settlement instantly, and if that stupid, unforgivable affair with Cromwell years ago came out—even if there wasn't anything in it—he'd file countersuit and I wouldn't have got a penny. I was almost out of my mind, John! And Vicki knew it.—But I've got the settlement now, and I'm a rich woman . . . Can't you just forget—"

I stepped back into Judy's room, sat down weakly and closed my eyes, and tried desperately, my brain whirling so that I could hardly think at all, to make some sense out of that. For a moment I thought the whole thing was clear in my mind, the way a blurred telescopic vision becomes suddenly sharp and focussed. Or could it be possible that Mrs. de Courcey . . . ? I thought about how she'd known Dex Cromwell was dead, when she came in that night, and her sidelong glance without so much as batting an eye at that bloodstained candle holder, and all the elaborate nonsense about how someone could get into Judy's room to plant the evidence against her, and that sudden change in her manner when she stepped out on the balcony and saw that Steve Ewing was in his room . . . Mary de Courcey . . . desperate, lonely, unnecessary—as she'd put it herself—even for appearances . . .

And Colonel Primrose? What would he do? What could he do?

I got up suddenly. I knew he was coming in to see me, and I didn't want him to find me there, for he'd know from my face, instantly, that I'd heard them. I picked up Judy's car keys and put on my hat, and started for the door. Just as I did, the telephone rang in my own room.

I hurried through to it and picked it up. For a moment I just stood there, listening in a kind of astonished stupor, not understanding the voice speaking to me. Then I recognized it. It was Wu Lung, the China boy at Dexter Cromwell's cottage up at Tahoe.

"Missy Latham? This Wu Lung," he repeated patiently. "Missy Latham? This Wu Lung.—Missy Bonner, he want you come light away, he have velly bad accident."

After that first instant it took me no time at all to hear the authentic note in that high, cheerful, sing-song voice; but it was a full long moment before I realized that he didn't mean Clem and he did mean Judy.

"You come light away," he said, and hung up.

I think the one thing I've learned from all the broken collar bones and arms and legs from football and the concussions from falling off horses that my young seem constantly to meet up with is not to work myself into a state of hysteria before I arrive on the scene. Nevertheless I don't think I ever got out of a room and downstairs into the lobby of any hotel as fast as I did just then. The problem of whether Colonel Primrose would compound a felony—if that's what the problem was—for an old sweetheart was as far from my mind as the right of an old sweetheart to kill the people who were blackmailing her.

I did, however, have a momentary qualm as I flew across the lobby and came face to granite face with Sergeant Phineas T. Buck standing in front of the dollar slot machine, one great hand coming methodically down on the lever. He gave me a glance instinct with fishy-eyed suspicion.

"Where's the Colonel, ma'am?" he asked, as if he were saying actually, "Fee, fie, foh, fum, I smell the blood of an Army man."

I didn't, as it turned out, have to tell him what his chief had no doubt quite pointedly not told him—that he was seeing Mrs. de Courcey. I'd just opened my mouth to say something hastily, I don't know what, when there was a metallic subterranean whir in the slot machine, like some Aladdin's djinn disgorging himself, and I saw the three bars level at the pointer, and the jackpot poured out, great silver cartwheels bounding and clinking and clattering on the floor of the Washoe lobby and rolling off into every corner like the cartoonist's picture of the taxpayers' money over the nation's farmers.

I wonder now what would have happened if Sergeant Buck hadn't been there . . . or if I'd been in less of a hurry to get away and had glanced into the cocktail lounge and seen Clem and Polly Wagner and asked them to go along up to Tahoe with me. But it's useless to consider that now, because I didn't even look that way, and they saw me only when they joined everybody else to help collect Sergeant Buck's rolling stock, as I fled through the door into the street.

26

I don't have any clear recollection now of that second trip up Mount Rose, except that I made it, lurching and skidding, in what seemed an age-long time and was considerably less than I'd ever dare do it again . . . knowing now that Death rode up there with me, silent and hollow-eyed at my side, and maybe even smiling as we got out of the car together by the corral behind the chalet, gleaming white against the sapphire blue of the mountain-girdled lake.

I hurried across the grass and the red-tiled terrace. The door was open, but nobody was in the pine-panelled room where the planes of golden sunlight streaming through the windows turned to scarlet as they reached the red leather chairs and sofas. But in another room I could hear Wu Lung's high-pitched voice.

I called "Judy! Judy!" and ran across the room, through the door by the rock fireplace.

Kaye Gorman was sitting at the end of the sofa. No one else was in the room.

"Where's Judy?" I cried. "What's happened to her?"

I was really and genuinely alarmed now.

"Judy? She's all right—nothing happened."

She shrugged her shoulders casually.

"It's just that hysterical Chinaman. She's gone back to Reno—you must have passed her. Did you come by Truckee?"

I sank down in a chair and dropped my hat on the floor, a great wave of relief relaxing my taut muscles.

"I came up Mount Rose," I said. "He said she'd had a bad accident."

Kaye shook her head. Her round baby face was turned

directly to me, so that only its creamy softness showed; but she was watching me, intently, and with the oddest expression in her delft blue saucer eyes . . . so odd in fact that my heart grew suddenly quite cold.

"Are you *sure* she's all right, Kaye?" I asked quietly.

"Oh, don't be silly. She just went off the road and got scared—that's all."

Her voice was perfectly casual and matter-of-fact . . . but something in the atmosphere so tense and alive and . . . wrong that I could almost feel it touching me made every nerve and fibre of my body suddenly taut and aware. I picked up my hat, moved to the edge of my chair and stopped, startled by the sudden jangling of the phone on the low table, just at the end of the sofa where Kaye was sitting, her small booted feet curled up under her, her hands thrust in the pockets of the pioneer pants she wore.

She made no move to answer it, but just sat looking at me. It rang again, urgently, it seemed to me, though I knew the urgency must be in my own bewildered mind. She still made no move.

"Are you going to answer that?" I asked practically. "Or shall I?"

A curious smile curled in two tiny lines at the end of her soft red mouth. The phone rang again, a long long time. She sat there, looking strangely at me, her eyes intent and searching. And then, as if she'd been making up her mind, and preparing in some way, and was ready now, her white hand with its long scarlet lacquered nails and a great star ruby on one finger, crept out and took up the phone.

And I heard—incredibly—Wu Lung's high-pitched sing-song voice coming from her heavily rouged lips:

"Hello. No—Missy Latham he come, but he go. He all time tly find Miss Bonner. Missy Bonner he gone long time, he gone Leno. Velly Okay."

And I just sat there, staring like some newly made petrifaction, unable to believe my ears.

She put down the phone and looked at me, her eyebrows raised ever so slightly.

"That was your friend Colonel Primrose," she said. "It's too bad, too.—He's just down at State Line—I heard the operator."

My heart gave a quick leap, and died again, as I began to realize, in some kind of an unconscious way, bewildered and frightened, what this meant.

I said—and I was vaguely conscious of being surprised that my voice should sound perfectly normal—"Are you *mad*, Kaye Gorman?"

A queer light, frightened and angry, flickered for an instant in her big blue eyes and was gone as she answered, with her steady hard-edged voice from which all the plush creaminess had vanished: "No. I'm not. I'm just not taking any more chances with you, Mrs. Latham."

I suppose any normally bright person would have realized, fully and consciously, at that point, what I utterly failed to realize except in a frightened and unthinking way. I sat there, staring at her. The only sound in the room was the lip-lap, lip-lap of the tiny waves on the sandy beach, and somewhere out on the blue sparkling water the long lengthening roar of a speed boat.

Then I started to get up—just thinking, I suppose, in my simple way, that I'd had enough of this and I might as well leave. There was a sudden hardening of Kaye Gorman's smooth face and a sudden movement of her hand. I stopped, staring at the small blue revolver she held resting on her knee.

"Sit down," she said.

I sat. I don't think it occurred to me to do anything else.

"And don't act like a fool. I want to know how many people you've told."

Her voice was as cold as a steel trap.

I suppose it would sound ridiculous to say that I wasn't afraid, then, when I was . . . afraid with a deeper, more profound fear than I've ever known it was possible to feel. But in some queer way I wasn't actually immediately aware of it, unless of course I was so aware of it that I was totally numbed. Or perhaps it was because it was so bizarre and incredible, and because I still didn't really understand, and genuinely didn't know what she was talking about, that I could do nothing but ask, blankly:

"Told . . . what?"

Her eyes narrowed sharply, her face flushed a hot angry red. She uncurled from her seat on the sofa and got abruptly to her feet.

"Look here, Mrs. Latham—if you think being funny, or stupid, is going to help you, you're wrong. *One more life's nothing to me . . .*"

And then, as it dawned on me, and I understood, in a way, without understanding why or how, I stared at her so utterly and I suppose so obviously dumbfounded, that she stood there for an instant, completely rigid, as if some violent electric shock had rooted her speechless to the rug. The awfullest kaleidoscope of doubt, fear, anger and then abject horror passed slowly through her eyes.

The blue muzzle in her hands wavered as she took a step toward me, her face perfectly ashen.

"You mean you didn't know I killed Dex Cromwell and Vicki?"

Each word dropped separate and distinct from her lips, not made of sound but of fear, tangible and distilled, as if all other quality had gone and only that was left.

I was too dazed to remember now, but I think I must have sat there, shaking my head back and forth. My hands still resting on the arms of the chair were lumps of ice.

Suddenly her body stiffened. She shot forward, her eyes burning into mine like hard blue coals.

"You're lying!" she whispered. "You're trying to fool me again!"

I whispered too: *"Again?"*

"Yes, again. I let you fool me once, into thinking you *had* made a mistake, you really did think it was me, not Vicki, with that dress—not because you're clever, Grace Latham, but because I couldn't figure out how you could have seen me . . . not till last night, and I sat at the table you were at and saw you could see the door of the powder room through the little glass at the top . . . That's when I knew you'd seen me . . . and that's what you meant when you screamed 'It's Kaye Gorman!' "

She straightened up and stared down at me, her voice quieter, but just as cold and inexorable.

"I know your sort. Were you likely to mistake a cheap piece of chantilly for a hand-made alençon? And you didn't fool me—I knew what you meant when you said 'I thought it was you,' trying to pretend you'd made a mistake!"

She stopped abruptly, her full mouth drawn to a thin cruel line. I found myself thinking vaguely that this must have been the way she'd looked when she found Clem's family had lost their money. The bitter contempt in her voice must have been the same, too, when she found she hadn't got what she'd married him for.

She looked down at the revolver in her hand.

I made a supreme attempt to control my nerves and my voice.

"Listen," I said. "You're absolutely crazy. I hadn't the faintest idea it was you—it's nothing but your guilty conscience that's making you read all that into what I said. But I suppose it doesn't make any difference, now, that I just happen to be one of those people that can't tell machine-made lace from any other, and hardly know one kind from another, and care less."

"You mean—Vicki hadn't told you that Dex told her all about a girl who lived at Tucker's while he was here before? Oh, he didn't mention her name, but Vicki put two and two together and made four. You mean she didn't tell you that?"

And quite suddenly I remembered Vicki in the hotel room just before Colonel Primrose came in, saying "Did somebody ever tell you a story, not mentioning names, but so you can put two and two together?"

I shook my head, but it was too late.

"I don't believe you, Mrs. Latham.—She told someone. She told me she had, so she'd be safe, she said."

I know I had the desperate vague idea that I ought to go on talking, to keep her talking, if I could.

"I still don't know why you did it . . . were you in love with Dexter Cromwell?"

She gave a quick curious laugh that was almost a sob.

"I certainly was not. It doesn't matter to you. That's my business."

"It's my business to know why you tried to make it appear that Judy did it."

She laughed again.

"It would be yours if they weren't going to find you up here after I've left, so everybody's going to think you did it yourself to save your niece. And it's simple, anyway—she was a natural."

She'd taken a step toward me, the pupils of her eyes black pin points in the great blue irises, her hand tightening on the blue gun, its muzzle bigger and more terrifying as I tried to keep my eyes on her eyes, not on it.

"And you'll do just as well. Nobody knows I'm here. My car's hidden down the road, I've got an alibi. They're going to find powder burns on your face and your fingerprints on this gun. And they'll hush it up—Reno doesn't like scandal, it hurts business."

She took a step toward me, and another. I could feel my heart pounding painfully in my throat. Every other part of me was paralyzed. Even then, I can remember thinking, like an impartial and quite detached spectator, that from her point of view at least it was pretty ingenious. Next to Clem and Judy, I had the greatest motive for getting rid of Dex Cromwell, and I'd seen Vicki going down toward the District Attorney's office.

She was quite close to me, and I closed my eyes. Except for her voice and the pounding of my own heart, there was no sound, except that lip-lap, lip-lap of the waves outside. I've wondered sometimes, especially since I've known Colonel Primrose, what I'd do if I knew absolutely that I was going to die—whether I could face it with dignity, or whether I'd go all to pieces. Now, as death came step by step closer to me, guided by a hand that knew none of the civilized vir-tures of mercy, or honesty—nothing but overweening ambition and pride—I found myself waiting perfectly motionless and relaxed, with no thought at all in my mind but that I wouldn't want my two children to think I'd taken my own life . . . or for Colonel Primrose to think so.

Kaye Gorman had crossed the white bearskin rug. I could hear her booted foot touch the pine floor, not a yard from my chair.—And just as it did, suddenly and quite grotesquely I heard someone whistling, outside by the corral.

My heart gave a great leap. The cold shadow of the blue steel lifted from my face. I opened my eyes as I heard the sharp stifled intake of Kaye's breath. She was standing motionless there.

The whistling stopped abruptly. I heard footsteps on the terrace, and a voice, young and pleasant, call out, "Hi, Wu Lung—you here? Can I borrow the halter on the corral post?"

I opened my mouth to scream. The revolver rose instantly to within ten inches of my face. "Don't you make a sound or it'll be both of us!" Kaye Gorman whispered. She took a step back and turned half-way toward the door, and I heard Wu Lung's voice rise from her mouth:

"Velly okay. Missy Clomwell she no want long time."

The man laughed. "I'll bring it back tomorrow."

Then I heard his steps going back across the tiled terrace, and my heart died with them. He was still whistling merrily, and I sat there, the blue muzzle of the revolver just by my face as she stepped silently back toward me, wondering rather idly how long he would stay, knowing she couldn't shoot me while he was out there . . .

The whistling stopped suddenly, and the man began to sing.

Kaye Gorman's face was very white. She caught her full red lower lip in her teeth, and still keeping that gun pointed square at me, took three quick steps to the door.

The singing voice still went on cheerfully outside.

"What in God's name is he doing?" she whispered, and I realized with a start of surprise that she wasn't cool and cold-blooded any more. She came back and sat down on the sofa again, across the rug from me, the revolver never wavering . . . and I saw then, utterly incredibly, for the singing voice outside had never stopped an instant, the door behind Kaye Gorman opening very slowly, and then looming in it the huge circus-garbed figure of Sergeant Phineas T. Buck.

I don't know what happened then. I only saw the sharp flash of fright in Kaye's blue eyes as she saw my eyes fastened behind her. I could feel myself fading slowly out as she leaped to her feet and whirled around, and then sprang past me toward the door, and I can only vaguely remember Sergeant Buck's clearing the sofa in one gigantic stride, and the bearskin rug going neatly out from under his feet as he landed on it, and his terrific crash onto the pine floor. The last thing I heard was a bitterly emphatic string of old Army expressions, and the first thing I remember after that was opening my eyes and closing them again, knowing I was safe, and that the arms tight around me were Colonel Primrose's, and the lips whispering, "My dear, my dearest!" against my forehead, where the cold blue steel had almost touched, were his too. I was vaguely aware that in some way the singing young man had been his device, but I was still far too dazed to realize that I had been part of a trap, and that Sergeant Buck was quite right when he said that Colonel Primrose would gladly hang his own grandmother—if and when the necessity arose.

27

I didn't go back to Reno, not that day. Judy and Polly came up . . . Judy who hadn't been anywhere near Tahoe, and who, in one of those Hardyesque coincidences, had actually been going up to her apartment in the elevator just as I slipped down the stairs by it, to avoid Colonel Primrose if he'd come out of Mrs. de Courcey's room while I was waiting.

I went down with them, around the lake and by way of Carson City. We turned in the road beyond the Bowers', where a sign in the shape of the golden sun with a ring-necked squirrel sitting on it pointed to Polly's ranch, nestling in the pine trees at the foot of the smooth dun-colored hills. A couple of Basque shepherd dogs asleep on the wide verandah got up and barked once, and came to greet us, wagging their lovely tails. A cowboy on a pinto pony, with a small boy in chaps and a big Western hat hanging stoutly on to the pommel, ambled past us and waved to Polly. The smell of the pines, and the white curl of smoke rising from the cook house, and the odor of lamb stew and coffee coming out of it with the clatter of dishes, were perfectly divine and sane and ordinary. And over it all, the pine trees and the half-acre of sunflowers and lupin and scotch broom beyond the row of old lombardy poplars, was a peace and homeliness that I wouldn't have thought could exist less than fifteen miles from the Boulevard of Broken Dreams, with its clatter and jangle and bars and gambling and all its raggle-taggle tinsel glamor.

We went to Polly's cottage, not far from the ranch house. It was a minute log cabin with a fire place and maple furniture and hooked rugs, all cozy and homey and the sort of place it would be fun to spend six weeks in even if one wasn't getting a divorce. And it was there that evening, when the hot sun went down behind the mountains across the valley, and Polly and Judy and I had finished supper that the China boy brought on a tray for us, and lighted a log fire, for it gets cold out on the desert at night, that Colonel Primrose and Sergeant Buck came.

"You'll never forgive me, will you?" Colonel Primrose said. He sat down beside me on the sofa, with a rueful smile. "If I'd had the faintest idea she'd misunderstood that cry of yours when we found Vicki . . ."

He shook his head.

"As a matter of fact, I hadn't thought you could be in any definite danger, not till I called and heard that imitation China talk.—I spent six years out there, and she wasn't really very good at it anyway. Well, I saw something was up then, and realizing that Buck and I would be pretty late—I called up that lad at the garage. And I told him not to go inside, because—to be quite frank with you—I didn't want Mrs. Gorman to get alarmed and make a getaway. And he couldn't locate the place right away, so Buck and I got there at just about the same time."

He shook his head again, very soberly.

"And of course, one of the most curious things about this whole business was that she didn't remember she was across the state line, and make a play about extradition . . . since being across that line was the salient point in Cromwell's murder."

I suppose I looked puzzled, or maybe only just as I'd looked ever since I first decided to come to Reno, as I can't, off-hand, think of any moment since I arrived there that I hadn't been puzzled about something, in one degree or another.

"Did she get away?" I asked.

His face was grave as he lighted his cigar with a rush from the basket on the hearth.

"In a sense. She got away through the trees to her car— she'd hidden it along the road—and headed back to Nevada. Buck picked her up near Brockway. She stayed ahead of him all the way up Mount Rose . . . and went off the road, where the sharp turn is. Doing about seventy."

I realized then, of course, why they'd sent us around

through Carson, instead of letting us come the shorter way, over the mountain. In my mind's eye I could see again that curve on the narrow rock-strewn road where Clem and I had skidded, and the sunny valley of the Washoe, two thousand feet below us down the sheer brown rock walls. I closed my eyes. I could see, quite easily, Kaye's car racing madly around that sharp bend, and failing . . . so that she paid in one swift awful instant—eternally and irrevocably, according to the oldest law of justice—a life for a life . . . except that this was one life for two lives.

We sat silently a moment, gazing into the fire.

"Why did she do it?" Judy said at last, her voice scarcely louder than a whisper.

But before Colonel Primrose could answer we heard a car come into the ranch yard and a tap at the door. Sergeant Buck opened it; and his face congealed to a more glacial frigidity than it had ever done even for me as Mrs. de Courcey came in, handsome and smartly gowned. Clem Bonner followed her.

Mary de Courcey sat down across the room, and Clem stood by the high chintz-draped window, his pipe in his hand, his dark sombre eyes fixed on the bright nimbus of Judy's head, glowing against the flames. She didn't look at him, and my heart sank, further even than it had done at Lake Tahoe as I waited to join the ranks of the inglorious dead.

"My dear, I think it's perfectly marvellous you escaped at all!" Mrs. de Courcey's voice babbled. "It must have been simply harrowing—mustn't it, John?"

Sergeant Buck, standing by the door, gave her a glance as warm—to use one of his own expressions—as Muley's goose nine days dead. Colonel Primrose smiled at me.

"If hereafter you'll only do as you're told . . ." he said placidly.

"Do you mean you actually knew it was Kaye who'd done this, when I saw you up at Tahoe this morning?" I demanded.

He nodded.

"Positively and without a doubt," he said. "And I might as well tell you about it—and not just as a sort of concluding formality. There's still a complication or two in this business."

His eyes rested with an amused twinkle on Judy, and on Clem.

"Out at that Tahoe service station I needed just two things: the date of Mrs. Gorman's arrival in Reno three years ago, and the date of her divorce. And, to a lesser degree, the date of her second marriage."

Judy turned sharply in her chair, her gray eyes questioning.

"For that was the whole and entire point of this," Colonel Primrose went on calmly. "As you all know, the only thing that gives a Reno divorce a semblance of validity is the six weeks' residence. Well, Mrs. Gorman came here on July 11th, got her decree at 2:30 on the afternoon of August 22nd, and married Jake Gorman at 2:40 the same day. She had Clem's power of attorney, and there was no trouble about anything.

"I was interested in two general points from the outset. It seemed to me very odd that Mrs. Gorman should have come back to Reno. She had secure possession of nearly a million and a half, her former husband's wife meant nothing to her, and she had no way of knowing that her former husband would be here. Her coming back was very strange on the face of it . . . for the Kaye Gormans of this world burn their bridges. They don't like people to see how rickety they were. They obliterate their trails—they don't come back on them.

"The second point that interested me was that piling up of evidence against Judy Bonner . . . the cunning that was too cunning. I thought—if some of you will pardon me—that it pointed from the beginning to a woman. At the same time it didn't appear there was any woman here who had a particular reason for animosity toward Judy. And in fact that Mrs. Gorman really had none was one of the things that made this so infernally diabolical."

He stopped to relight his cigar.

"All this was complicated by Vicki's death—and in a sense made clear by it. For wherever we looked, we ran across that curious little man Mr. Tucker. He was the key to the situation, actually. There was no connection between him and Cromwell, but there he always was, just the same . . . and I began to think he had some connection with Cromwell's murderer. When Vicki was killed I saw generally what it was all about. She wasn't here three years ago, but she had one advantage over the rest of us—she knew Mr. Tucker. And knowing him, she figured one thing out . . . much too neatly for her own good—namely, the motive for the murder. And I looked up the obvious point, and found that Kaye Gorman had lived at Mr. Tucker's boarding house when she got her divorce.

"Well, after Cromwell had got his divorce, in July of the year Mrs. Gorman was here, he lived for some time up at that cottage at Tahoe—on the California side. I went up there . . . and the puzzle fitted together in a flash. There's a China boy there—about sixty years old—and by good luck he'd been there for some years. I showed him a group of photographs of people I thought had been Cromwell's guests."

I saw poor Clem Bonner's face flush darkly. I couldn't help glancing at Judy. She was sitting there, in riding clothes that she wears even better than she does a dance frock, bending forward looking at the fire, enchantingly lovely, her gray eyes sun-flecked like forest pools under her long gold-tipped lashes and burnished hair . . . and blissfully unconscious of what Colonel Primrose was bound to say—that she had been up there, too long, with the man she had planned to marry . . . at a time, as the Archbishop of Canterbury said in a more impressive connection, when she was not in a position to entertain a proposition of marriage.

"And he recognized the first picture I showed him," Colonel Primrose went on, with a calm that I was far from sharing, and that seemed to me even a little callous. "He said, 'that's Mrs. Bonner, she stayed week-ends with Cromwell.' "

28

Judy Bonner stared at him, her jaw dropping, a look of such perfect denial in her eyes that I was still more shocked, some way, than I'd been before.

Colonel Primrose chuckled a little.

"It would have been rather . . . misleading, if anyone had been listening in," he said. "For it was Kaye Gorman's picture I was showing him. Of course he recognized her as Mrs. Bonner—she *was* Mrs. Bonner, when she spent those week-ends there. And that must have been when she was getting her decree, because, as you know, at this time she hadn't been here weekends . . . she came on Monday."

I sank back against the cushions, suddenly, and very much ashamed of myself. Clem's face flushed again as my eyes met his. Then I looked at Judy . . . she must put two and two together, I thought, and see what Clem had been thinking. And I saw, looking at her, grave and innocent and attentive, that she hadn't—the idea had simply never occurred to her.

"And by the way, Clem—what did you go up to Tahoe for?"

"Kaye told me Cromwell said he had a letter of Judy's, that wouldn't let her change her mind about marrying him," Clem said shortly. "She told me where to find it. I supposed that's what Judy had been up there for, the night I got back."

Judy's eyes darkened indignantly. "That's not true! I . . . did go after a letter, but not that sort! And anyway, it was gone. A . . . a friend of mine had already got it. But I didn't know that then."

It would be wrong to describe Sergeant Buck's face as just red. It was the color of a maple sugar bucket that had been polished and allowed to tarnish again.

Polly Wagner giggled irrepressibly.

"Ah well," Colonel Primrose said hastily, "I'm afraid Kaye was using the old business of discrediting her successor. Well, I knew then, of course, what it was all about. Mrs. Gorman had spent one or more week-ends out of Nevada—and one was enough. She hadn't made up her time, her divorce was obtained on perjured evidence, on her own part and on that of her witness—one Mr. Tucker. The penalty for perjury in the state of Nevada is from one to fourteen years in the state penitentiary.

"One person, of course, knew all that—namely Mr. Dexter Cromwell. Well, at one-thirty Tuesday morning, when someone called for Mrs. Bonner's car, Mr. Tucker was under the eye of about eleven young women. That left Mrs. Gorman . . . and she had far more to lose than Mr. Tucker. There was the perjury penalty in either case. In Mrs. Gorman's case there was also the fact that she'd just raked in about a million and a half dollars on false pretenses: namely, the false pretense that she was the wife of Jake Gorman. She had one of three things to do. She could pay blackmail to Cromwell all her life, she could give up her million and a half, or she could get Mr. Cromwell out of the way. I imagine two of those things didn't occur to her very seriously.

"Well, she and Cromwell had plenty to talk about, that night. It's even quite possible that Cromwell suggested a drive, and that Kaye—knowing Reno, and Cromwell—suggested the race track, where they'd be undisturbed. They left the River House and went by the hotel. She went in, ostensibly to go up to her own room; learned, from Whitey, probably, just as Mrs. Latham did, that Judy was out. She knew Mrs. Latham had gone home, tired from her trip, to go to bed. She went up to Judy's room—probably by the corridor window, the fire escape and the balcony windows—got the candle holder, the shirt and the hairs, and put in the call for Judy's car. It was while she was up there that Clem had his scene with Cromwell, who, of course, was waiting for her in his car alone. Clem left, and Kaye came out of the hotel, I'd imagine by the service entrance so as not to be seen. She and Cromwell went out to the race track. After she'd killed him she ran back to where the garage man had left the car—everybody in the hotel uses that garage, by the way, and they were leaving the key under the rubber mat even when Kaye was out here last. She drove the car back to Island Street, near the Washoe, saw Judy in the bar, between two and two-thirty, went up to Judy's room again and planted the shirt and the weapon in the clothes hamper . . . being careful, naturally, not to get blood on Judy's car or on herself. Well—it was desperate and opportunist, but it succeeded, up to a point."

Colonel Primrose's black parrot eyes twinkled as he looked at me.

"And so," he said, very urbanely, "we come to the only glimmer of joy and good will in all this painful business. Namely, that Mrs. Bonner of course doesn't have to go on with her divorce action."

And Judy stared at him, only half comprehending, and so did I.

"It's purely a routine matter for the family lawyer.—Kaye Gorman's divorce from Clem Bonner was quite illegal, her marriage to Jake Gorman was quite illegal. And consequently Clem Bonner's marriage to Judy Carroll was quite illegal. In short, Mrs. Bonner, you are Mrs. Bonner . . . only by courtesy. You not only don't have to get a divorce—you can't. Well, it does simplify matters, doesn't it?"

There was the oddest silence in the little room, Clem Bonner and Judy staring at each other for the first time. And Polly Wagner giggled again, and started to speak, and stopped just as Judy recovered herself.

"It . . . it does, rather, doesn't it?" she said. She pushed her bright hair back from her forehead with a bewildered little gesture. "I mean . . . it means we've never been married? We've just been . . . just been living in sin . . . like they do in the movies!"

Clem Bonner came slowly across the room from the window, his lean brown face breaking into a grin of the kind I'd remembered, that made him really recognizable to me for the first time since he'd come to Reno. But even as he grinned there was no mistaking the depth of feeling in his voice.

"Miss Carroll," he said gravely, "I'm ashamed of you.—And I want you to come down to the court house with me, right away . . . and let me make an honest woman out of you."

Judy looked at him, her gray sunflecked eyes dancing behind their long lashes, a smile trembling in the corners of her red mouth.

She took a step toward him. "I always knew you'd do the right thing by me, Mr. Bonner . . ."

The door closed behind them, alone together at last . . . but it was a long time before we heard them move, out there in the desert night. And it was not very long after that that Clem came racing back.

"We've got to have witnesses!" he shouted.

Mrs. de Courcey jumped up. "Oh, lovely!" she cried. "Oh, isn't it charming! Isn't it *charming*, John! Come on!"

Clem dashed out again. Mary de Courcey stood expectantly by the door. For a moment or two a combat that if it had been on an Olympian scale would have shaken the universe to its foundations waged there in Polly Wagner's room. I realized, in a flash of intuition, that Sergeant Buck, faithful unto death, was not allowing any woman to get his colonel at a marriage license bureau with a pen in his hands.

I held my breath . . . and Fate materialized in the room, in the charming shy young form of Polly Wagner. She looked at Sergeant Buck, and at Colonel Primrose, and at me. Then she got up, went over to the door, and took both Mary de Courcey and Sergeant Buck firmly by the arm.

"Let's us go," she said. "They're going to need somebody with *influence,* to get a license this time of night."

"Okay, miss," Sergeant Buck said.

He came to what was in effect, if not in fact, a smart attention, just barely failed to salute, held the door open, and followed Mrs. de Courcey and Polly out into the night.

I looked at Colonel Primrose, and then I laughed until I ached, and after a moment he laughed too. Then he said, very soberly, "I came up to your room, you know, just to tell you to keep away from Kaye. But Mary de Courcey got hold of me. She'd got herself in rather a jam."

I nodded.

"I overheard her talking to you," I said. "I really thought, in kind of a vague way, that she'd done it herself—telling you she was rich now, and asking you to forget . . ."

He was looking at me so oddly that I stopped. He shook his head, smiling.

"She was only asking me to forget she'd married de Courcey and not me, twenty years ago," he said.

"And . . . marry her now?" I asked.

"Something of the sort."

"And . . . are you?"

He shook his head. "There's only one woman, my dear," he said, very earnestly . . . and that's as far as he got. There was a crashing knock on the door, and Sergeant Buck came in.

"You're wanted outside a minute, sir," he said.

If that iron face had ever expressed an emotion, there was a faint tinge of satisfaction on it at that moment.

Colonel Primrose's black eyes snapped. But after all, one doesn't go through West Point for nothing. He got up, nodded to me and went out.

Sergeant Buck closed the door solidly, and stood firmly planted with his massive back against it. I knew now exactly how Steve Ewing had felt, locked alone with him, before the woman in the room below had heard the crash of breaking furniture. My heart sank. Sergeant Buck looked too much like a gray desperate fortress ringed around with besiegers whose numbers were growing and whose methods were becoming more insidious.

He cleared his throat, his face turning that odd tarnished color. We had, I knew, Sergeant Buck and I, come at last to a showdown.

"I want to state, ma'am," he said, out of one corner of his mouth, "that I'm against the Colonel marrying."

"Of course, Sergeant," I said hastily. "I quite understand."

He cleared his throat again. The brassy hue of his granite visage deepened alarmingly.

"I want to state further, ma'am," he said, with a menacing glare, "if, irregardless of what's good for him, he's bound to get himself married . . . why, maybe it'd better be you than some other people."

He then nodded stiffly, and started out. And I recovered, I think, in remarkably short time, considering everything.

"You . . . you're just . . . making the best of a bad job, Sergeant," I managed to say.

He stopped, his face brightening for an instant, as if he had been trying to find some way of putting it.

"That's it, ma'am," he said, gratefully.

Then his face congealed again.

"No offense meant, ma'am."

"None taken, Sergeant," I said.

He opened the door. In the headlights of Clem's car I saw Colonel Primrose coming back to the cottage.

"Good-night, ma'am," Sergeant Buck said, grimly.